COLLECTED
ESSAYS OF
# Joel S.
# Goldsmith

# COLLECTED ESSAYS OF
# Joel S. Goldsmith

DeVorss & Company
P.O. Box 550, Marina del Rey, CA 90294-0550

Printed in the United States of America

# Contents

These essays were originally
published as separate booklets.

*Except the Lord build the house, they
labour in vain that build it.*

Psalm 127

Illumination dissolves all material ties  and binds men
together with the golden chains of spiritual understanding;
it acknowledges only the leadership of the Christ; it has no
ritual or rule but the divine, impersonal universal Love; no
other worship than the inner Flame that is ever lit at the shrine
of Spirit. This union is the free state of spiritual brotherhood.
The only restraint is the discipline of Soul, therefore we know
liberty without license; we are a united universe without
physical limits; a divine service to God without ceremony or
creed. The illumined walk without fear—by Grace.

From *The Infinite Way* by Joel S. Goldsmith.

# Supply

## PART I

THE SECRET OF SUPPLY is to be found in Luke 12:22–32.

"And he said unto his disciples, Therefore I say unto you, Take no thought for your life, what ye shall eat; neither for the body, what ye shall put on.

"The life is more than meat, and the body is more than raiment.

"Consider the ravens: for they neither sow nor reap; which neither have storehouse nor barn; and God feedeth them: how much more are ye better than the fowls?

"And which of you with taking thought can add to his stature one cubit?

"If ye then be not able to do that thing which is least, why take ye thought for the rest?

"Consider the lilies how they grow: they toil not, they spin not; and yet I say unto you, that Solomon in all his glory was not arrayed like one of these.

"If then God so clothe the grass, which is today in the field, and tomorrow is cast into the oven; how much more will he clothe you, O ye of little faith?

1

"And seek not ye what ye shall eat, or what ye shall drink, neither be ye of doubtful mind.

"For all these things do the nations of the world seek after: and your Father knoweth that ye have need of these things.

"But rather seek ye the kingdom of God; and all these things shall be added unto you.

"Fear not, little flock; for it is your Father's good pleasure to give you the kingdom."

The question now arises: how is it possible to "take no thought" for money when pressing obligations must be met? How can we trust God when year in and year out these financial problems confront us, and usually through no fault of our own? We have seen in these passages from Luke that the way to solve our difficulties is to take no thought for supply, whether of money, food, clothing or any other form. And the reason that we need have no anxiety about these things is that "it is your Father's good pleasure to GIVE you the kingdom" because He "knoweth that ye have need of these things."

In order that we may enter wholly into the Spirit of Confidence in this inspired message of Scripture, we must understand that money is not supply but is the result or effect of supply. There is no such thing as a supply of money, clothes, homes, automobiles or food. All these constitute the effect of supply, and if this infinite supply were not present within you, there never would be "the added things" in your experience. The added things, of course, are those practical things like money, food and clothing that are so necessary at this stage of our existence.

Since money is not supply, what is? Let us digress for a moment and look at the orange tree which is laden with fruit. We know that the oranges do not constitute supply because when these have been eaten, or sold, or given away, a new crop starts at once to grow. The oranges are gone but the supply remains. Within that tree there is a law in operation. Call it a law of God or a law of nature—the name of the law is not too important, but the recognition of the presence of a law operating in, through or as the tree—is important. That law operates to draw in through the roots the minerals, substances, elements of air, water and sunshine which it (the law) then transforms into sap that is drawn up through the trunk of the tree and distributed through the branches and finally sent into expression as blossoms. In due time this law transforms the blossoms into a green marble and this becomes the full-grown orange. The orange is the result or effect of the operation of the law acting in, through and as the orange tree. As long as this law is present we will have oranges. The orange of itself cannot produce another orange. Thus we understand that the law is the supply and oranges are the fruits, the results or the effect of the law.

Within you and within me there is also a law in operation —a law of life—and our awareness of the presence of this law is our supply. Money and the things necessary for daily living are the effects of the consciousness of the activity of the law within. This understanding enables us to take thought off the things of the outer world and abide in the consciousness of the law.

What is the law which is our supply? The universal or divine Consciousness, your individual consciousness, is this law. This law actually is your consciousness. Thus your consciousness becomes the law of supply unto you, producing its own image and likeness in the form of those things necessary to your well-being. As there is no limitation to your consciousness, there is no limit to your conscious awareness of the action of the law and therefore no limit to your supply in all its forms.

Divine or universal Consciousness, your individual consciousness, is spiritual. The activity of this law within you is likewise spiritual and therefore your supply in all its forms is spiritual, infinite and everpresent. What we behold as money, food and clothing, automobiles and homes, represents our concepts of these ideas. Our concepts are as infinite as our mind.

Let us agree now to see that as we need take no thought for oranges as long as we have the source or supply which is continually producing fruit for us, so we need no longer take thought about dollars. Let us learn to think of dollars as we do of leaves on trees, or oranges, as the natural and inevitable result of the law active within. There is truly no need to be concerned even when the trees appear to be bare, as long as we are conscious of the truth that the law is even now operating within to bring forth fruit after its own kind. Regardless of the state of our finances at any given moment, let us not be concerned or worried because we now know that the law acting in, through and as our consciousness is at work within us, when we are asleep as well as when we are awake, to provide all those added things.

Let us learn to look at the lilies and rejoice at the proof of the presence of God's love for His creation. Let us watch the sparrows and note how confidently they trust this law.

Let us rejoice when we see the flowers in Spring and Summer because they assure us of the divine Presence. As we learn to enjoy the beauties and bounties of nature, with no desire to hoard any of them, and with no fear that there is less than an infinite supply of them, so learn to enjoy the fruitage of our infinite supply—the results of that infinite storehouse within us—with no fear of any lack to plague us.

Enjoy these things of the outer realm but do not consider them as supply. Our conscious awareness of the presence and activity of the law is our consciousness of supply, and the outer things are the forms our consciousness takes on. The inner supply appears as the necessary outer things.

## PART II

WE SAY IN ONE BREATH take no thought for your supply or for your health, and in the next breath we say you must "pray without ceasing" and "ye shall know the truth, and the truth shall make you free." Though seeming to be contradictory, both admonitions are correct, but they have to be understood.

There is always a belief of human good in operation—a law of averages, and from this we derive our material benefit. In house-to-house selling, there is usually an average of one sale out of twenty calls; in advertising through circulars, there is an average of returns of about 2%; in automobile driving, it is claimed a certain percentage of accidents is the rule; life insurance companies have a table of life expectancy, and they can tell you any year how many years you will continue here—as an average.

Now to live humanly—that is, to go along day to day *letting* these averages affect you, letting the human beliefs operate upon you—is not scientific living. This is all the belief of human existence, and unless you specifically do something about it, you bring yourself under these so-called economic or health laws, which actually are but beliefs or suggestions. These suggestions are so universal as to become mesmeric in their operation and act on those who are not alert, and bring forth limitation.

What must we do to keep ourselves free of these suggestions, so that we can live above them? First, we must live on a higher plane of consciousness. So far as possible, we must train ourselves mentally to know that anything that exists in the realm of effect is not cause, is not creative, and has no power over us. This brings up the important metaphysical point that I am the law, I am Truth, I am Life eternal. Since I am infinite consciousness, since I am the law, then nothing in the external can act upon me and be a law unto me. There is nothing from which we can ever suffer but the acceptance of illusion as Reality. These things called sin and disease are not what we are suffering from, they are the forms the one error assumes. Regardless of the name you use, they are hypnotism, suggestion, illusion, appearing as person, place or thing —appearing as sin, disease, lack and limitation.

We must not live as though we were effect with something operating upon us. Let us remember to live as the law, as the Principle of our being. You can only take possession of your affairs as you consciously realize that they are the effect of your own consciousness; the image and likeness of your own being; the manifestation or expression of your divine Self— then alone can you be a law unto them.

We must begin our days with the inner reminder of our true identity. We must identify ourselves as Spirit, as Principle, as the law of Life unto our affairs. It is a very necessary thing to remember that we have no needs; we are infinite, individual, spiritual consciousness embodying within ourselves the infinity of good; therefore, we are that center, that point of God consciousness which can feed five thousand any day and every day—not by using our bank account, but by using the infinity of good pouring through us the same as it poured through Jesus. We do not meet people with the idea of what we can get or what they can do for us, but we go out into life as the presence of God. During the day, whether doing housework, driving cars, selling or buying, we must consciously remember that we are the law unto our universe, and that means that we are a law of Love unto all with whom we come in contact. Consciously remember that all who come within range of our thought and activity must be blessed by the contact, because we are a law of Love; we are the Light of the world. Consciously remember that we do not need anything, because we are the law of supply in action—we can feed five thousand of those who do not yet know their identity.

There is a belief of separation between us and God—our good—and this we correct by realizing, "I and my Father are one"; "All that the Father hath is mine"; "the place whereon I stand is holy ground." In the recognition of the infinity of our being, we realize the truth of the Bible; we realize the truth of these promises; they are no longer quotations, but statements of fact, and that brings us to the point of demarcation between "knowing the truth" and "taking no thought." We are realizing truth now as an established truth within our own consciousness—the truth of our being. We are not taking thought to make any good come to us; we are not giving ourselves a treatment to make something happen to us; but we are realizing the truth, knowing the truth of our own identity, of our oneness with the infinite, with our infinite capacities. The reason for realizing and knowing this truth is that through the ages we have come to be known as man—as something other than God-being—and unless we now consciously and daily remind ourselves of the true nature of our being, we will come under the general belief that we are something separate and apart from God.

There is a belief that we are separate from some people who are really a part of our completeness; a belief that we are separate or apart from certain spiritual ideas necessary to our fulfillment, and these may appear as persons, papers, home, companionship, opportunity. This we correct by realizing that our oneness with God constitutes our oneness with every idea. Illustrative of this is the telephone. Through my telephone I can reach any other telephone any place in the world, but I cannot reach even my next-door neighbor by telephone without first going through the central station. Then by establishing my oneness with central, I am one with every telephone. In the realization of our oneness with infinite Principle, Love, God, we find and manifest our oneness with every idea necessary to the unfoldment of our completeness.

Never forget that you cannot live scientifically as man or idea, but that you must realize yourself to be Life, Truth and Love. You must accept Jesus' revelation of the I AM until it becomes realization with you.

Stop trying to apply Truth; applying Truth is the action of the human thought—there is nothing to apply Truth to. Truth is infinite, therefore there is nothing to which we can apply Truth. It is the reality of being and there is nothing inside or outside for Truth to act upon—Truth is self-acting, self-operative.

We are all engaged in activities through which our supply appears to come. Regardless of whether it is a business, a profession, or an art, it is an activity of Mind and Life. So regarded, our activity is intelligently and lovingly directed and sustained. It is even more than this: As an emanation of Mind, it is Mind itself individually appearing and expressing its own being, nature and character. The government is upon Its shoulder, and Mind alone is responsible. We learn to let go and let Mind assume its responsibilities.

In the Bible we read the trials and tribulations of Elijah. As we follow him through the 18th chapter of 1 Kings, we must understand that only the consciousness of the presence of Spirit, God—within him—could have done these mighty works. No human power can accomplish them.

In the 19th chapter, we find discouragement creeping in at what appears as the failure of Elijah's ministry. Actually this is an opportunity to prove that the power is not that of a human but actually is God-power acting as what appears as a man, but really is God appearing as an individual.

The food prepared for Elijah under the juniper tree is his own awareness of the presence of God appearing in tangible form.

We are led in this 19th chapter of 1 Kings to the great message in the 18th verse, "Yet I have left me seven thousand in Israel, all the knees which have not bowed into Baal, and every mouth which hath not kissed him." You note here that God has not saved seven thousand for Elijah, but for Himself —for God appearing as Elijah.

Whatever our work may be—in business, in a profession, or as an artist—God, the Mind of the individual, always has kept seven thousand (completeness) for Himself, and as we learn to listen for that still small voice which spoke to Elijah, we too will be led to where our work and recognition and compensation are to be found. You exist as individual Mind, therefore, all that is necessary to your fulfillment is included in the infinite consciousness which you are.

In an individual way, God is expressing Itself as you, and your abilities are really the abilities of God; your activity is actually the activity of Mind, Life; and, therefore, the responsibility for you is God's responsibility. Gain this consciousness of God's presence and you have the whole secret of success in every walk of life.

As individual spiritual consciousness, there are seven thousand (fulfillment) prepared for you—that is, God, the Mind of the individual, the Mind of you, has given you your individual abilities and capacities and likewise has given you the opportunity and the rewards. These appear to fit each situation.

Always remember that God, the Mind of you, has prepared for you all that is necessary for the fulfillment of your individual experience. You are never outside the harmony of God's being. Cultivate the consciousness of the presence of God every moment.

It is our conscious union with God which enables us to live without taking thought and makes possible a life of complete abundance—"by Grace."

There is an invisible bond between all of us. We are not on earth to get from one another, but to share the spiritual treasures which are of God. Our interest in each other is, in Truth, purely spiritual. Our purpose in life is the unfolding of the Spirit within.

From the height of spiritual vision we do not look upon each other as man and woman; as rich or poor; as grand or humble. All human values are submerged in our common interest to seek and find the Kingdom within. We see each other as travellers on the Path of Light; we share our unfoldments, our experiences, and our spiritual resources. We would not withhold any of these from each other.

Likewise, there is no envy or jealousy of each other's spiritual attainments. Let us even for a moment realize that whatever we possess of supply, position, prestige or power, health, beauty or wealth is the gift of God and, therefore, equally available to all of us in the measure of our openness of consciousness—and you understand how we can carry our impersonal love out into the human world.

Let us once catch the vision that whatever anyone possesses, even of what appears as material good, is but the expression of their state of consciousness, and it would be impossible to envy any of another's possessions, or even to desire them. The first step in living by Grace, living in universal peace, must begin with the understanding that all anyone has is of the Father; that is, all that we possess and all that we can ever own is the outpouring of our own infinite consciousness.

We are all "joint heirs with Christ in God," therefore, we all draw upon the resources of our own infinite Mind and Soul, and we need not labor, strive or struggle for that which is already divinely ours. All that anyone possesses at any time, even of what seems to be of human value, is the unfoldment of their own state of consciousness and, therefore, belongs only to the possessor. That which we have is the result of fruitage of our own state of consciousness, and what we have not yet achieved, is our own lack of conscious union with God— our infinite Consciousness.

We can have as much of everything as we desire by enlarging the borders of our understanding and realization. Nothing that we can get from another would ever really be ours, even if we received it legally. It would still belong only to the one with the consciousness of it. What is yours is eternally yours and only because it is your state of consciousness in expression.

"All that the Father [my very own infinite consciousness] hath—is mine."

The realization of this Truth would enable all men to live together in one world harmoniously, joyously, successfully —without fear of each other and without greed, envy or lust. We would be back in the Garden of Eden. We would live without taking thought—which is by Grace. This would constitute the recognition of life as the gift of God—as the free flow of our consciousness. It would reveal the invisible spiritual tie which binds us in an eternal brotherhood of Love. It would forever solve the problem of supply and thereby establish the reign of peace on earth.

# Metaphysical Healing

HEALINGS ARE ALWAYS in proportion to our understanding of the truth about God, man, idea, body. Healing has nothing to do with someone "out there" called a patient. When anyone asks for spiritual help or healing, that ends their part in what follows until they acknowledge their so-called healing. We are not concerned with the so-called patient, the claim, the cause of the illness or its nature, nor with his sins or fears. We are now concerned only with the truth of being—the truth of God, man, idea, body. The activity of this truth in our consciousness is the Christ, Saviour or healing influence.

Failure to heal is the result of much mis-knowledge of the truth of God, man, idea, body, and this mis-knowledge stems primarily from orthodox religious beliefs which have not been rooted out of our thought. Few realize to what extent they are blinded by superstitious orthodoxy.

There is only one answer to the question, What is God? and the answer is I AM. God is the Mind, the Life of the individual. Any mental hedging or inner reservation on this subject will result in ultimate failure. There is but one universal I, whether it is being spoken by Jesus Christ or John Smith. When Jesus revealed: "He that seeth me seeth him that sent me," he was revealing a universal Truth or Principle. There must be no quibbling about this. You either understand this truth or you do not—and if you do not there is no need for you to seek any further reason for failure to heal. The revelation of Jesus the Christ is clear. "I am the way, the truth, and the life." Unless you can accept this as a principle, therefore as the truth about you and about every individual, you have no foundation upon which to stand. The truth is that God is the Mind and Life of the individual. God is the only "I."

Next comes the question, What is man? and the answer is that man is idea, body, manifestation. My body is idea, or manifestation. Likewise my business, home, wealth—these exist as idea or manifestation, expression, reflection. For this reason and for no other my body is the exact image and likeness of my consciousness and reflects or expresses the qualities, character and nature of my own consciousness of existence.

So far, then, we understand that "I" am God; that God is the Mind and Life of the individual; that my body exists as the idea of God. God, or I AM, is universal, infinite, omnipotent and omnipresent; therefore, the idea body is equally indestructible, imperishable, eternal. It was never born and will never die. I shall never be without the conscious awareness of my body; therefore, I shall never be without my body.

When we look out upon the world with our eyes we are not beholding our bodies, we are not seeing this infinite divine idea body, we are beholding a more or less universal *concept* of the idea. As we see a healthy body, a beautiful flower or tree, we are seeing a good concept of the idea body, flower, tree. When we see an aging, ailing body or withered flower or decaying tree, we are beholding an erroneous concept of the divine idea. As we improve our concepts of idea, body, manifestation, we term this improving of concepts *healing*. Actually nothing has happened to the so-called patient or his body —the change has come in the individual's consciousness and becomes visible as improved belief or healing. For this reason the healer alone must accept responsibility for healing and never try to shift the blame for non-healing onto the person who asked for help. *That individual* is I AM, Life, Truth and Love, and his body exists as perfect spiritual eternal harmonious idea subject only to the laws of Principle, Mind, Soul, Spirit—and it is our privilege, duty and responsibility to know this truth, and the truth will make free every person who turns to us.

As individual, infinite spiritual consciousness, I embody my universe, I embody or include the idea body, home, activity, income, health, wealth, companionship, and these are subject only to spiritual law and life. The body is not self-acting; it is governed harmoniously by spiritual power. When the body appears to be discordant, inactive, overactive, changing, paining, it is always the belief that the body is self-acting; that it of itself has the power to move or not move, to ache, pain, sicken or die. This is not true. The body is not self-acting. It has no intelligence or activity of its own. All action is Mind action, therefore omnipotent good action. When we know this truth, the body responds to this knowing or understanding of Truth. No change then takes place in the body because the error never was there. It is entirely exchanging a concept for the truth that already is, always has been and ever will be. Remember there is no patient "out there" and no body out there to be healed, improved or corrected. Always it is a false concept or belief to be corrected in individual thought.

When we begin to understand that the body is not self-acting; that it responds only to the stimulus of Mind, we can disregard so-called inharmonious bodily conditions and abide in the truth that Life is forever expressing itself harmoniously, perfectly and eternally as the divine idea, body.

The understanding that I AM—individual infinite spiritual consciousness embodying every right idea and governing them harmoniously—brings forth health, harmony, home, employment, recognition, peace, joy and dominion. The understanding that this is true of every individual dispels the illusion of hate, enmity, opposition, etc. This also makes of you a practitioner, a healer, a teacher, whether or not professionally engaged in the work.

We come now to face our orthodox superstitions and to leave them. Was Jesus sent into the world by God to save it from sin, disease, or slavery? No. God, the infinite Principle, Life, Truth and Love, knows no error, no evil, no sin and no sinner. Jesus so clearly apprehended this truth that this apprehension became the Saviour, Healer, Teacher even as it will in you. *The activity of Truth in individual consciousness is the only Christ.* No person is ever the Christ. The activity of Truth in individual consciousness constitutes the only Christ, the ever-present Christ who was ''before Abraham.'' The activity of Truth in your consciousness is the Christ of you. The activity of Truth in the consciousness of the Buddha revealed the nature of sin, disease and death to be illusion or mirage. The activity of Truth in the consciousness of Jesus Christ revealed the nothingness of matter; it unfolded as a Healing Consciousness before which sin and disease disappeared and death was overcome. Every erroneous concept, whether of body or business, health or church, must disappear as the right idea of these appear in individual and collective consciousness.

What about immaculate conception or spiritual birth? The immaculate conception or spiritual birth is the dawning in individual consciousness of the activity of Truth or the Christ idea. It appeared in Jesus as the revelation that "I am the way, the truth, and the life"; "I am the resurrection and the life"; "He that seeth me seeth him that sent me." The activity of Truth in my consciousness, the Christ of me, is revealing that I am individual, infinite, spiritual consciousness embodying my universe, including my body, my health, wealth, practice, income, home, companionship, eternality and immortality.

Let the activity of Truth in your consciousness be your first and last and only concern, and the Christ of you will also reveal itself in an individual, infinite Way.

There is no evil. Let us therefore stop the resistance to the particular discord or inharmony of human existence which now confronts us. These apparent discords will disappear as we are able to cease our resistance to them. We are able to do this only in proportion to our realization of the spiritual nature of the universe. Since this is true, it is evident that neither heaven nor earth can contain error of any nature, and therefore the unillumined human thought is seeing error in the very place where God shines through; discord where harmony is; hate where love abounds; fear where confidence really is.

The work on which we have embarked is the realization that we are individual infinite spiritual consciousness embodying within ourselves all good. This is the song we will sing, the sermon we will preach, the lessons we will teach, and until realization comes, this is our theme, our motif. It is the silver cord of Truth running through every message.

Nothing can come to you; nothing can be added. You are already that place in consciousness through which infinity is pouring. That which we term your humanhood must be still so as to be a clear transparency through which your infinite individual Self may appear, express or reveal itself.

When we view Niagara Falls from the front, we might assume that it could run dry with so much water continually pouring over the Falls. Looking behind the immediate scene, we behold Lake Erie, and realize that actually there is no Niagara, that this is but a name given to Lake Erie at a point where Erie pours over the Falls. The infinity of Niagara Falls is assured by virtue of the fact that actually the source of Niagara, that which constitutes Niagara, is really Lake Erie.

So with us. We are that place where God becomes visible. We are the Word made flesh. Our source, and that which constitutes us, is God—infinite divine Being. We are God-being, God-appearing, God-manifesting. That is the true glory of our being.

The story is told of Marconi, that when he was very young, he told friends that he would be the one to give wireless to the world and not the many older seekers who had been experimenting for years. After he fulfilled his promise he was asked why he had been so certain that he would succeed. His answer was that the other scientists were seeking first to discover a means to overcome resistance in the air to the messages that would be sent through the air, whereas he had already discovered there was no resistance.

The world is fighting a power of evil; we have discovered there is no such power. While materia medica seeks to overcome or cure disease, and theology struggles to overcome sin, we have learned there is no reality to disease or sin, and our so-called healings are brought about through this understanding.

We know that there are these human appearances called sin and disease, but we know that because of the infinite spiritual nature of our being, they are not realities of being; they are not evil power; they have no Principle to support them; therefore, they exist only as unrealities accepted as realities, illusion accepted as condition, the misinterpretation of what actually is.

We bind ourselves by believing there is power outside of us—power for good or for evil. All power is given to *you*. And this power is always good because of the infinite source whence it flows. The recognition of this great fact brings a peace and a joy untold, yet felt by all who come within range of your thought. It makes you beloved of men. It brings you recognition and reward. It establishes you in the thoughts of men and becomes the foundation of an eternal good will.

Whenever you are faced with a problem, regardless of its nature, seek the solution within your own consciousness. Instead of running around here and there; instead of seeking an answer from this or that person; instead of looking for the solution outside of yourself—turn within. In the quiet and calm of your own mind, let the answer to your problem unfold itself. If, the first or second or third time you turn in peace to the kingdom within, you fail to perceive the completed picture, try again. You will not be too late, nor will the solution appear too late. As you learn to depend on this means for the working out of your problems and experiences, you will become more and more adept in quickly discerning your mind's revelation of harmony. Too long have we sought our health, peace and prosperity outside ourselves. Now let us go within and learn that there is never a failure nor a disappointment in the whole realm of our consciousness. Nor will we ever find delays or betrayals when we find the calm of our own Soul and the presence of an infinite Principle governing, guarding, guiding and protecting every step of our journey through life.

Do not be surprised now when the outstanding truth unfolds to you that your consciousness is the all-power and the only power acting upon your affairs, controlling and maintaining your health, revealing to you the intelligence and direction necessary for your success in any and every walk of life. Does this astonish you? No wonder! Heretofore you have believed that somewhere there existed a deific power, a supreme presence, which, *if you could reach it,* might aid you or even heal your body of its ills. Now it becomes clear to you that the universal Mind or Consciousness is the mind of the individual man and *it* is the all-power and ever-presence which can never leave you nor forsake you, and it is "closer than breathing." And you need not pray to it, petition it or in any way seek its favor; you need but this recognition leading to the complete realization of this truth. From now on you will relax and *feel* the constant assurance of the presence and power of this illumined consciousness. You can now say, "I will not fear what man shall do unto me." No more will you fear conditions or circumstances seemingly outside of you or beyond your control. Now you know that all that can transpire in your experience is occurring within your consciousness and therefore subject to its government and control.

Nor will you ever forget the depth of feeling accompanying this revelation within you, nor the sense of confidence and courage that immediately follows it. Life is no longer a problem-filled series of events, but a joyous success of unfolding delights. Failure is recognized as the result of a universal belief in a power outside of ourselves. Success is the natural consequence of our realization of infinite power within.

Release from fear, worry and doubt leaves us free to function normally, healthfully and confidently. The body acts immediately from the stimulus coming to it from within. New vitality, strength and bodily peace follow as naturally as rest follows sleep. Little do we know of the depth of the riches within us until we come to know the realm of our own consciousness, the kingdom of our mind.

When we become still and go into the temple of our being for the answer to some important question, or the solution of a vital problem, it is well that we do not formulate some idea of our own, or outline a plan, or let our wish in the matter father our thought. Rather should we still the thinking mind so far as possible and adopt a listening attitude. It is not the personal sense of mind (or conscious mind) which is to supply the answer. Nor is it the educated mind or the mind formed of our environment and experience, but the universal Mind, the Reality of us, the creative Consciousness. And this is best heard when the senses and reasoning mind are silent.

This inner Mind not only shows us the solution to any problem and the right direction to take in any situation, but, being the universal Mind, it is the consciousness of every individual and brings every person and circumstance together for the good of the whole.

Obviously we cannot look to this universal Consciousness to work with us for anyone's destruction or loss. What is accomplished in and through the kingdom of our mind is always constructive individually and collectively. It can therefore never be the means of harm, loss or injury to another. Nor do we direct our thought at another, or project it outside ourselves in any direction. That which our mind is unfolding to us is, at the time, operating as the consciousness of all concerned. We need never concern ourselves with "reaching" some other mind, or influencing some other person. Remember that the activity of Mind unfolding as us is the influence unto all who can possibly be affected by or concerned in the problem or situation. There are no unsolved problems in Mind, and this same Mind which is our own consciousness is the only power necessary to establishing and maintaining the harmony of all that concerns us. It is our turning within that brings forth the answer already established. Our listening attitude makes us receptive to the presence and the power within us. Our periods of silent contemplation reveal the infinite force and constructive energy and intelligent direction always abiding in us. Thus we discover in our mental realm the Aladdin's Lamp. Instead of rubbing and wishing, we turn in silence and listen—and all that is necessary for the harmony and success of life flows forth abundantly, and we learn to live joyously, healthfully, and successfully—not by reason of any person or circumstance outside ourselves, but because of the influence and grace within our own being.

No longer is it necessary to try to dominate our business associates or members of our family. The law within us maintains our rights and privileges. Every right desire of our heart is fulfilled now and without struggle or strife, without fear or doubt. The more we learn to relax and quickly contemplate our real desires, the more quickly and more easily are they achieved. It is not required of us that we suffer our way through life or strive endlessly for some desired good—but we have failed to perceive the presence of an inner law capable of establishing and maintaining our outer welfare.

It seems strange to us at first to realize that inner laws govern outer events—and it may at first appear difficult to achieve the state of consciousness wherein these laws of our inner being come into tangible expression. We will achieve it, however, in proportion to our ability to relax mentally; to gain an inner calm and peace; and therein quietly contemplate the revelations which come to us from within. Quietness and

confidence soon bring us face to face with Reality, the real
laws governing us.

Lest the question should arise in your thought as to how a
law operating in your consciousness (and without conscious
effort or direction) can affect individuals and circumstances
outside yourself, let me ask you to watch the result of your
recognition of the inner laws and learn this through observation.

We are yet to become aware of the fact that we embrace
our world within ourselves; that all that exists as persons,
places and things lives only within our own consciousness.
We could never become aware of anything outside the realm
of our own mind. And all that is within our mental kingdom
is joyously and harmoniously directed and sustained by the
laws within. We do not direct or enforce these laws; they eternally operate within us and govern the world without.

The peace within becomes the harmony without. As our
thought takes on the nature of the inner freedom, it loses its
sense of fear, doubt, or discouragement. As the realization of
our dominion dawns in thought, more assurance, confidence
and certainty become evident. We become a new being, and
the world reflects back to us our own higher attitude toward
it. Gradually an understanding of our fellow man and his
problems unfolds to us from within, and more love flows out
from us, more tolerance, cooperativeness, helpfulness, and
compassion, and we find the world responds to our newer
concept of it, and then all the universe rushes to us to pour
its riches and treasures in our lap.

Many fine treaties and covenants have been signed by
nations and men, and nearly all have failed, because no document is any better than the character of those who administer
it. When we become imbued with the fire of our inner being,
we no longer need contracts and agreements in writing because
it becomes first nature with us to be just, honest, intelligent

and kind—and these qualities are met in all those who become part of our experience in the home, office, shop, and in all our walks of life. The good revealed in our consciousness returns to us, "pressed down, shaken together, and running over."

In this new consciousness we are less angered by the acts of other people; less impatient with their shortcomings; less disturbed by their failings. And likewise, instead of being hampered and restricted by external conditions, we either do not meet with them or else brush right by them with but little concern. We realize that something within us is ruling our universe; an inner presence is maintaining outer harmony. The peace and quiet of our own Soul is the law of harmony and success to our world of daily experience.

All that has gone before this is as nothing unless you have seen that over and above all "knowing the truth," you must be overshadowed by the Christ.

When the Christ dawns in individual consciousness, the sense of personal self diminishes. This Christ becomes our real being. We have no desires, no will, no power of our own. The Christ overshadows our personal selfhood. We still perceive in the background this finite sense and at times it tries to assert itself and even dominate the scene. "For the good that I would I do not: but the evil which I would not, that I do," says Paul.

But let it be clear to you that the personal self cannot heal, teach or govern harmoniously. It must be held in abeyance that the Christ may have full dominion within our consciousness.

The work that is done with the letter of Truth, with declarations and so-called treatments, is insignificant compared with what is accomplished when we have surrendered our will and action to the Christ.

Christ comes to our consciousness most clearly in those

moments when we come face to face with problems for which we have no answer, and no power to surmount, and we realize that "I can of mine own self do nothing." In these moments of self-effacement, the gentle Christ overshadows us, permeates our consciousness and brings the "Peace, be still" to the troubled mind.

In this Christ we find rest, peace, comfort and healing. The unlabored power of spiritual sense possesses us, and discords and inharmonies fade away as darkness disappears with the coming of light. Indeed, it is comparable only to the breaking of dawn; and the gradual influx of divine Light colors the scenes in our mind and dispels one by one the illusions of sense, the darker places in human thought.

The stress of daily living would deprive us of this great Spirit unless we are careful to retire often into the sanctuary of our inner being and there let the Christ be our honored guest.

Never let vain conceit or a belief in personal power keep you from this sacred experience. Be willing. Be receptive. Be still.

# Meditation

To MEDITATE IS "to fix the mind upon; think about continuously; contemplate; to engage in continuous and contemplated thought; dwell mentally on anything; ruminate and cogitate."

In the spiritual tongue meditation is prayer. True prayer or meditation is not a thinking about ourselves or our problems but rather the contemplation of God and God activities, and the nature of God, and the nature of the world that God created.

Everyone should take some time daily to retire to a quiet spot for meditation. During this period he should turn his thought to God, and consider his understanding of God, and search out a deeper understanding of the nature of Spirit and its formations, and of Mind and its infinite manifestation. He should be careful not to take any of his ills or other problems into his meditation. This particular period is set aside, dedicated and consecrated to thinking about God and God's universe.

As God is the Mind and Soul of every individual, it is possible for all of us to be tuned in to the kingdom of God and receive the divine messages and assurances and benefits of the one infinite Love. The grace of God which we receive in these periods of meditation or prayer becomes tangible to us in the fulfilling of our so-called human needs. If we do not open our consciousness to the reception of spiritual understanding we must not be surprised if we do not experience spiritual good in our daily living, and there is no other way to open our consciousness to the realm of Soul than through meditation or prayer, through contemplating the things of God. "Thou wilt keep him in perfect peace whose mind is stayed on Thee."

All through the day our thoughts are centered on the activities of human experience, on family cares and duties and earning a livelihood, on social and community affairs, and sometimes even on greater affairs of state. Is it not natural then that at some time during the day or evening we take time off to retire to our inner consciousness, which is the Temple of God, and there dwell upon the things of God? Above all we must develop the sense of receptivity so that we can become ever more aware of the very presence of God in His Holy Temple which is our consciousness. In the secret place of the Most High, which is the Holy of Holies, which is our very own inner consciousness, we receive illumination, guidance, wisdom and spiritual power. "In quietness and confidence shall be my strength."

As we learn to listen to the "still small voice," the Spirit of God opens our consciousness to the immediate awareness of spiritual good. We are filled with the divine energies of Spirit; we are illumined with the light of the Soul; we are refreshed with the waters of Life and fed with the meat which does not perish. This spiritual food is never rationed to those who learn to meet God within the temple of their being.

To receive the grace of God we must retire from the world of sense, we must learn to silence the material senses and have audience with God. God must become to us a living reality, a divine presence, a Holy Spirit within, and this can only be when we have learned to meditate, pray, contemplate God.

Through meditation we become aware of the presence of the Christ, and this awareness remains with us all day and all night as we go about our human existence. This awareness enters into every experience and prospers every endeavor. This consciousness of the presence of Christ is a light unto our feet and a guiding star unto our aspirations. It is the presence that goes before us to make the crooked places straight. It is the quality in our consciousness that makes us understood and appreciated by others.

On awaking in the morning, and preferably before you get out of bed, turn your thought to the realization that "I and my Father are one"; "Son, . . . all that I have is thine"; that "The place whereon thou standest is holy ground." Then let the meaning of these statements unfold from within your own consciousness. Gain a conviction of your oneness with the Father, with the universal Life, the universal Mind, the universal Consciousness. Feel the infinity of good within you which is the evidence of your oneness with the infinite source of your being.

As soon as you begin to feel a stirring within you, or a sense of peace, or the surge of divine Life, then get out of bed and make your physical preparations for the day. Before leaving your home sit down and ponder your oneness with God.

The wave is one with the ocean, indivisible and inseparable from the whole ocean. All that the ocean is the wave is, and all the power, all the energy, all the strength, all the life, all the substance of the ocean is expressed in every wave. The wave has access to all that lies beneath it, for the wave really is the ocean as the ocean is the wave, inseparable, indivisible, one. And note here this very important point, that there is no place where one wave comes to an end and the next wave begins, so that the oneness of the wave with the ocean includes the oneness of every wave with every other wave.

As a wave is one with the ocean, so you are one with God. Your oneness with the universal Life constitutes your oneness with every individual expression of that Life; your oneness with divine Mind constitutes your oneness with every idea of Mind. As the infinity of God surges through you to bless all with whom you come in contact, remember that the infinity of God is also surging through every other individual on earth to you. No one is sharing anything with you that is of themselves, but all that they have is of the Father, so everything that you have is of the Father, and you are sharing it with all the world. You are one with the Father, with the universal Consciousness, and you are one with every spiritual idea of which this Consciousness is conscious.

This is a tremendous idea if you get it. It means that your interest is the interest of every individual in the world; it means that their interest is your interest; it means that we have no interest apart from each other even as we have no interest apart from God; it means actually that all that the Father hath is ours and all that we have is for the benefit of everyone else as everything that they have is for our benefit, and all for the glory of God.

Now this idea must unfold within you in an original way. It must bit by bit and day by day unfold in different ways, and always with greater meaning because of the infinity of Mind's ideas. You might note how a tree has many branches and how all of these branches are at one with the trunk of the tree and therefore with the root of the tree, and that the root of the tree is one with the earth and is drawing into it all that the earth possesses. And further, that each branch is not only one with the whole tree but each branch is one with every branch, connected parts of one whole. As you ponder this idea of your oneness with God and your oneness with every individual spiritual idea, new ideas along this line will unfold to you, new illustrations, original illustrations and symbols. By the time you have concluded this morning meditation you will find that you will actually feel the presence of God within you; you will actually feel the divine energy of Spirit; you will feel the surge of new life within you, and this too will lead on to other thoughts.

Whenever you leave one place to go to another place, such as leaving your home for business, or leaving your business for church, or going back to your home, pause for a second to realize that the Presence has gone before you to prepare the way, and that that same divine Presence remains behind you as a benediction to all who pass that way. At first you may forget to do this many times during the day, but by jogging your memory you will eventually find that this will become an established activity of your consciousness, and you will never make a move without realizing the divine Presence ahead of you and behind you; and in this way you will find yourself to be the Light of the world.

One of the subjects near and dear to us these past few years is that of peace, and we can have no faith in any perpetual peace based on whatever human documents or organizations can be formulated. True, they have their purpose and they are a necessary step for humans just as the Ten Commandments were a necessary step until the Sermon on the Mount replaced them with higher vision. You do not need the Ten Commandments because you need no admonition not to steal or lie or cheat, nor do you need any threat of punishment to keep you honest, clean and pure, but the Ten Commandments are necessary to those who have not yet learned righteousness for righteousness' sake. In the same way, the world is greatly in need of some kind of a human organization and some kind of human document to keep some form or some measure of peace in the world. But the real peace, the lasting peace, will only come as it has come to you individually through the realization that you do not need anything that the other fellow has and therefore there is nothing to war about. All that the Father hath is yours; what can you want besides that? As a matter of fact, as joint heir with Christ in God you could feed five thousand any day and every day without ever taking thought as to whence it should come.

When all mankind comes into this consciousness of its true identity there will be no wars, no competition, no strife. As you gain the full consciousness of your true identity, you show it forth in a greater sense of harmony, health and success, and one by one you attract others who are seeking the same way. In this way all men will ultimately be brought into the kingdom of heaven.

# Prayer

YE ASK, and receive not, because ye ask amiss," says the Apostle James. Have you ever thought of this when you have prayed for some time, and then found no answer to your prayer? "Ye ask amiss." There is the reason.

Prayer, when based on the belief that there is a need unfilled, a desire unsatisfied, is never in accord with true scientific prayer. A prayer for God to do something, send something, provide or heal, is equally without power.

It is sometimes believed that God requires a channel through which to fulfill our prayer; and this leads us to look outside ourselves for the answer. We may believe that supply can come to us, and therefore we watch for the person or position through which it is to come. We may be depending on a healer or teacher as the channel through which the healing is to come. "Ye ask amiss."

Any belief that that which we are seeking is anywhere but within *us*, within our very own consciousness, is the barrier separating us in belief from our harmony.

True prayer is never addressed to a Being outside ourselves, nor does true prayer expect anything from outside our own being. "The kingdom of God is within you," and all good must be sought there. Recognizing God to be the reality of our being, we know that all good is inherent in that Being, your being and mine. God is the substance of our being and therefore we are eternal and harmonious. God is Life, and this Life is self-sustained. He is our Soul, and we are pure and immortal. God is the Mind of the individual and this constitutes the intelligence of our being.

Rightly speaking, there is not God and you, but God is ever manifest *as* you and this is the oneness which assures you of infinite good. God is the Life, Mind, Body and Substance of individual being, therefore nothing can be added to any individual, and true prayer is the constant recognition of this truth.

Conscious awareness of our true being—of the infinite nature and character of our only being—this, too, is prayer. In this consciousness, instead of seeking, asking, waiting, in prayer, we turn our thought inward and listen for the "still small voice" which assures us that even before we asked, our Father knew and fulfilled the need. Here is the great secret of prayer, that God is All-in-all and God is forever manifested. There is no unmanifested good or God. That which we seem to be seeking is ever-present within us and already manifested, and we need to know this truth. All good already is, and is forever manifested. *The recognition of this truth is answered prayer.*

Our health, wealth, employment, home, harmony, etc., are then not dependent on some far-off God; are never dependent on a channel or person or place, but are eternally at hand, omnipresent, within our very consciousness, and the recognition of this fact is answered prayer. "I and my Father are

one," and this accounts for the completeness of individual
being.

Properly speaking, there is not God and you. It is impossible to pray aright unless this truth is understood. Prayer
becomes but blind faith or belief rather than understanding
when we do not know our real relationship with Deity. It is
our conscious awareness of the oneness of Being—the oneness
of Life, Mind, Truth, Love—that results in answered prayer.
It is the constant recognition of our life, our mind, our substance and activity as the manifestation of God-being that
constitutes true prayer. As we identify this God-being as the
only reality of our individual being, we are able to comprehend
ourselves as the fulfillment of God; as the completeness and
the perfection of being, all-inclusive, immortal and divine. The
recognition of the divinity of our individual being embracing
and including the allness of God is true prayer, which is ever-
answered prayer. The correction of the belief that we are ever
separate or apart from our good is the essence of true prayer.
*That which I am seeking, I am.* Whatever it is of good that I
have believed to be separate from me is, in fact, a constituted
part of my being. I include, embody and embrace within
myself, within my consciousness, the reality of God which
forms the infinity of health, wealth and harmony of my being.
The conscious awareness of this truth is true prayer.

Despite the Allness of God expressed as perfect individual
being, there constantly arise in human experience those ills
which call forth our understanding of prayer. What is the
nature of error, sin, disease? How can such things be *and God
be All-in-all?* Such things cannot be and are not, despite
the appearance of pain and discord and sorrow.

The Bible reveals to us the basic truth of being, namely,
that "God saw every thing that He had made, and behold, it
was very good." In this All-good that God made, there is

nothing that "defileth . . . or maketh a lie." And there is no other creative Principle. It becomes clear, then, that that which is appearing as error, sin, disease, pain and discord is illusion, mirage, nothingness.

Let us, then, as part of our prayer, remember that God made (evolved) all that was made, and in this universe of God there is only the All-Presence and All-Power of God, divine Love, and that therefore that which at the moment appears to us as error is a false sense of Reality.

There comes a time in our experience when spiritual inspiration reveals to individual consciousness a state of being free of mortal conditions and beliefs. Then we no longer live a life of mental affirmations and denials, but rather receive constant unfoldments of Truth from Mind. Sometimes this comes through no other channel than our own thought. It may come through a book or lecture or a service imparted by divine Consciousness. Regardless of the seeming channel through which it may come, it is Mind revealing itself to individual consciousness.

As we become more and more consciously aware of our oneness with the universal or Christ Mind, whatever desires or needs come to us bring with them their fulfillment of every righteous thought and wish. Is it not clear, then, that our oneness with Mind being established "in the beginning" through the relationship forever existing between God and His manifested being, it requires no conscious effort to bring about or maintain? The awareness of this truth is the connecting link with divine Consciousness.

To many, prayer means supplication and petition to a God in a place called heaven. That this prayer has resulted so universally in failure to attain its ends must prove that this is not prayer and that the God prayed to is not there listening. Human thought eventually realized the lack of answer to such prayers and turned to a search for the true God and the right concept of prayer. This led to a revelation of Truth as understood and practiced by Christ Jesus and many earlier revelators.

Here we learn that "the kingdom of God is within you" and therefore prayer must be directed within to that point in consciousness where the universal Life, God, becomes individualized as you or as me. We learn that God created (evolved) the world in the beginning and that "it was good." Being good, the universe must inevitably be complete, harmonious and perfect, so that instead of pleading for good, our prayer becomes the realization of the omnipresence of good, and so the higher concept reveals prayer as the affirmation of good and the denial of the existence of error as Reality.

When the prayer of affirmation results in the use of formulas it has a tendency to revert to old-fashioned faith-prayer and thereby loses potency. When, however, one's prayer consists of spontaneous and sincere affirmations of the infinity of God and of the harmony and perfection of His manifestation, one is indeed nearing the absolute of prayer, which is communion with God.

Before our enlightenment in Truth we prayed for things and persons. We sought to gain some personal end. With his great vision Emerson wrote: "Prayer that craves a particular commodity, anything less than all good, is vicious." Then this wise man defines prayer for us: "Prayer is the contemplation of the facts of life from the highest point of view. It is the soliloquy of a beholding and jubilant soul. It is the spirit of God pronouncing His works good. . . . As soon as the man is one with God, he will not beg." Prayer must not be understood as going to God for something, for, as Emerson continues, "Prayer as a means to effect a private end is meanness and theft."

Well, now we know what prayer is not and have glimpsed

that prayer is the union of our self, the individual Soul, with God, the universal Soul. Actually the individual Soul and the universal Soul are not two, but one, and the conscious awareness of this truth constitutes the union or oneness which is true prayer.

Jesus said, "My kingdom is not of this world," and this we must remember when we pray. To go to God carrying some recollection, some demand, some desire of this world, must end fruitlessly. When we enter our sanctuary of Spirit, we must leave outside all worldly wishes, needs, and lacks. We must drop "this world" and go to God with but one idea— communion with God, union or oneness with God. We must not pray to gain, to have something changed or corrected.

Prayer which is conscious oneness with God always results in bringing forth harmony, peace, joy, success. These are the "added things." It is not that Spirit produces or heals or corrects matter or the physical universe, but that we rise higher in consciousness to where there is less matter and therefore less discord, inharmony, disease or lack.

Communion with God is true prayer. It is the unfoldment in individual consciousness of His Presence and Power, and it makes you "every whit whole." Communion with God is in reality listening for the "still small voice." In this communion, or prayer, no words pass from you to God, but the consciousness of the presence of God is realized, as the impartation of Truth and Love comes from God within to you. It is a holy state of being and never leaves us where it finds us.

# Business

Business always seems to be dependent on certain conditions, circumstances and seasons, or on the good will of other persons. In the human picture business is affected by weather, finances, changing modes and fads, but turning from this picture we find that in reality business is the continuous activity of Principle; that this activity is infinite and harmonious, and that it is maintained and sustained by Principle itself.

Christian metaphysics, revealing the spiritual nature of business, aids us to lift our thoughts regarding all commercial activity to the place where the true idea of business is apprehended. Every idea, and your business is an idea of Mind, is supported by the animating Principle of the idea. "When an idea begins to work in thought, it furnishes all that is necessary for its equipment, establishment and nourishment."

—Adam Dickey

BUSINESS IS AN INFINITE activity, is forever without limit, and is never dependent on person, place or thing. Right where you are, business is. It is a result of and resident in individual consciousness, because individual consciousness is the universal Consciousness individually expressed. If we go about our tasks doing those things that lie nearest at hand, with faith that there is an ever-present, invisible power which the Hebrews call Emmanuel, or "God with us," and which Christians call the Christ, our work will always bear fruit.

This omnipresent and omnipotent power is the Presence of God prospering all right endeavor. It is only the degree in which we believe that it is either some personal effort of our own or another's, or that it is the good will of humans that prospers us, that causes apparent failure or lessening of fruit-ful activity. The prophet Isaiah clearly reminds us to "cease ye from man, whose breath is in his nostrils: for wherein is he to be accounted of?"

The point to remember is that at all times, and in all places, there is an invisible and omnipotent power acting to support every right human effort; and the way to demonstrate this is to recognize and acknowledge the presence and power of God and rely on it.

Business, spiritually understood, is the reverse of the usual conception in which every thought must be held to profit and loss and good policy and bad policy, or that which is or that which is not "good business." This business is never at the mercy of times and tides or circumstances and conditions, but is the free flow of the activity of Mind universally expressed.

Lack and limitation exist only in the belief that God and man have become separated from each other. The true under-standing of man's relationship to God reveals the ever-pres-ence of supply, the immediate availability of good in every form and in an unlimited quantity.

Spiritual truths cannot be intellectually discerned, yet they may be unfolded to our consciousness as the result of understanding thoughts received from the intellect. Before we can understand the meaning of at-one-ment with God, we must learn of our real relationship to Life, and for this purpose we may use a material symbol, as, let us say, a diamond.

Every cut diamond has numerous facets. Not only is it true that each facet is part of the diamond, but actually there can never be any separation between the facet and the diamond, because the diamond and the facet are one, one piece, one object, one whole.

If you can visualize the relationship between the facets and the diamond, you will, even though faintly, catch a glimpse of your inseparability from God. You will note that every facet expresses the life, fire, color and quality of the whole diamond; that each facet reflects the purity and the quality of the gem; and that the entire activity and all the beauty and durability of the stone are expressed in each individual facet, and never is any single facet detached or detachable from the whole gem. Beauty, color, fire, character, quality and strength are inherent in the diamond, and it expresses each and all of these attributes through every facet. The facet, then, is the outlet for the shining forth of the gem's brilliancy.

In like manner the supply of life, health, substance, strength and purity, which are the constituted qualities of divine Mind, are forever being expressed by Mind through each and every idea, man and the whole universe.

The facet of the diamond need not pray for color or brilliance because the diamond has no power to withhold these from its outer surface. This illustration makes plain why Spirit cannot withhold its supply of life, its quality of substance, activity and peace, from its individualized being.

Everything needful for the brightness and permanency of

the facet is within the stone and is forever expressing itself. All that man can ever need is within the universal Mind, eternal Life, and is pouring itself into expression through man every moment.

In the case of the diamond it is only necessary to keep the surface of the stone, the facets, clean—and the fire within shines forth in its perfection. In the case of man he needs only to keep his thought clear of the mists of fear and doubt—and the infinite supply inherent in his being will pour forth in abundant measure.

Too much effort is made by metaphysicians to *establish* at-one-ment with God, when the fact is that man can no more be separated from God, Love, Life, Mind or supply than the facet of the gem can be separated from the whole stone or any of its qualities. Man is forever at-one with his good, God; he needs but to know it. Nor can the life, substance or harmonious activity of Mind be withheld from any of its individualized expressions if we rest in the consciousness of our true relationship with the source of our good.

# Salesmanship

SCIENTIFIC CHRISTIANITY has revealed to human thought the present possibility of health and success. It has shown us how to think and live so as to individualize the power of Spirit, God, and how to utilize the laws of Mind with which to establish and maintain the harmony of mind, body and business.

One of the outstanding facts learned through the study and application of Truth to human affairs concerns the subject of salesmanship. All our earthly experiences involve to some extent the ability to sell. Many are actively engaged in selling commodities or services as a means of earning a living. The understanding of Truth is of vital importance to these "ambassadors of trade," as salespeople are often called.

We ordinarily think of selling as the disposition of goods or services to another for a sum of money or for some other form of trade. The best salesman is believed to be the one who can dispose of the most goods, or secure the highest prices for his product. These goals are attained in various ways, some of them ethical, others called "high-pressure salesmanship" which would not be considered in a business conducted according to the Golden Rule.

The student of Truth would always be the most successful salesman if he rightly understood and applied the laws of Mind in his work. Christian scientific selling can never meet with failure. It knows no "bad seasons" or "rainy weather" or "unseasonable weather" or any other of the innumerable excuses or alibis that are frequently given instead of orders.

The beginning of our understanding, or the starting point, is this: There is but one Mind, and this Mind is the Mind of individual man. Therefore the Mind of the buyer is the Mind of the seller; the Mind of the customer is the Mind of the storekeeper; the Mind of the designer, the manufacturer, the wholesaler, retailer and ultimate consumer is one and the same Mind, the ONLY Mind, individually expressed.

The importance of this fundamental understanding becomes clear when we learn that in this one Mind was conceived the idea which we desire to sell, and where also the idea was brought to fruition. This Mind operating in the customer recognized the good in your product, thereby completing the transaction, or rather, it reveals the transaction as already complete in Mind AND IN MANIFESTATION.

The belief that there are separate minds is the devil in salesmanship as it is also in every other phase of human experience. This belief in many minds leads us to the presumption that salespeople must convince the prospective buyer of the merits of their product. They sometimes misrepresent or exaggerate in order to sound convincing, and all this because of the mistaken belief that the Mind of the prospect is other than the Mind of the seller. When it is understood that the ONE Mind is operating as all parties, it becomes plain to us that in this Mind there are no conflicting interests, no opposing thoughts, no interfering persons or circumstances. In this oneness of Mind no one idea can interfere with another; no one idea can hinder the right development and progress of another.

This prepares us for the unfoldment of the next step: What are ideas? Metaphysics explains all that exists does so as ideas. It claims that sun, moon, stars, planets, plants, animals and man exist as ideas—ideas of the one Mind, God. It shows that these ideas are emanations of Mind and "live and move and have their being" in God, Mind. In this Mind or infinite Consciousness exists individual man and all that pertains to him. In this Consciousness is embraced the idea of business, of invention, of art and the sciences. This Consciousness includes also the various manifestations of weather, seasons and climates. Modes and methods of trans-process of thought are revealed to human apprehension.

Mind, the source of all intelligence, is necessarily intelligent in its action, and therefore all the ideas of Mind are held in harmonious relationship to other ideas. From this it can readily be seen that one idea of Mind, let us say weather, could not act as a hindrance to another idea, business. Also, as each idea is dependent on its source, Mind, for existence and continuity, it is clear that the idea, business, can in no wise be dependent on any other idea for its good. Individuals, likewise, are dependent on God, divine Love, only and can never be dependent on payroll, on the good will of persons, or the whims of circumstance. No sale of a legitimate product can be at the mercy of prejudice, bribery, ignorance or personality.

Salesmen sometimes have problems regarding rightful remuneration for their services. Here also it is necessary to remember that there is one Mind, and in this Mind there is no false activity, no selfish or dishonest thought or deed; that this Mind does recognize the true value of every idea. From this Consciousness only comes the proper reward or compensation for all right endeavor, and we need never look to person for this recognition or reward.

In presenting a proposition of any rightful nature we should hold to the truth that we are not presenting it to "man whose breath is in his nostrils," but to Mind. This Mind individualized as man is your prospect, your customer, your employer or employee. Trusting in the infinite nature and character of Mind, God, we find revealed all good in Mind's ideas. Relying on the integrity of the divine Being, we encounter this quality in individual man, the perfect image and likeness of eternal Being. This Principle reveals to us that whatever we recognize and acknowledge as the qualities and character of divine Love we find manifested in Love's reflection, individual man and the universe. The Truth we realize as pertaining to Mind we experience in manifestation, because "I and my Father are one."

# "Ye Are the Light"

## PART I

JESUS SAID: "Ye are the light of the world." Do you believe this? If you are the light, is there any darkness in you at all? If you are the light, can any light be added to you? Are you not the light—full and complete and bright? "I am the light of the world"—and ever will be—and if you accept this teaching you will shine as the noon-day sun in which is no darkness at all. "I am the light" will not permit question of why or wherefore. It accepts itself as the full radiance of the risen sun. "I am the light" seeks not for light, health, wealth, success, progress, but knows "I am." That which I am seeking, I am.

Jesus never said: "I will be resurrected," but he did say: "I AM the resurrection"—I am the power itself. He never spoke of seeking Truth, using Truth, applying Truth, but he said: "I AM the Truth." And remember he not only said "I am the light" but also "*Ye* are the light of the world." "Greater works shall ye do." Is all this true? Do you accept the truth "I am the truth"? When you abide steadfastly in this consciousness, all the petty trials and the big problems of human existence fade away because to Truth there is no error—to Life there is no death.

Sing within yourself, morning, noon and night, "I am the life, the truth, the light." Let a song of joy and grateful recognition surge through your being and know that the divine Being is your *only* being. This Being is all-inclusive life, love, substance, law and reality. You do not any more get at-one with Truth, or seek some truth with which to meet a need, but you realize with infinite joy, "I am the truth."

"Ye are the light of the world." As you rest in this consciousness, you will no longer find it necessary to overcome evil—destroy error—wrestle or rise above error. *As* the light, there is no "above" or "below"—you fill all space. *As* the light, darkness vanishes as you approach it and you have no consciousness of the darkness that has been dispelled, not any more than intelligence can be aware of the ignorance it displaces.

As there is but one Mind, remember that your thoughts, feelings, emotions are constantly being broadcast to the world. The world does not read your mind so as to be consciously aware of specific thoughts; nevertheless, it is attracted or repelled (without being consciously aware of it) by the general tenor of your thinking. Therefore, let your consciousness be filled with forgiveness, joy. Behold the universe as it is, sharing, cooperating, understanding. Constantly be the eternal Giver in action—not merely giving what is deserved, or earned, or won, but giving because the need appears; giving regardless of the so-called worthiness of the individual. Keep your consciousness free of judgment, criticism, condemnation, doubt, fear, discouragement. Think and voice error as little as you can. Consciously control your thought in the direction of I AM: "I" am the light; "I" am supply; "I" am intelligence; "I" am free.

This I AM is the universal Being, your Christ-Self; your true identity, the only one you have.

We speak of "your" life, "my" life, or "his" or "her" life, whereas it is necessary for us to remember that there is in all the world only ONE Life. This Life is deathless, ageless, diseaseless and changeless; it is the individual expression of that ONE divine Life. In other words, divine Life is our life. It contains no element of matter, discord or inharmony, no decomposition or decrepitude. This Life, which we are, is composed of the substance of Spirit, is infinite, eternal and harmonious.

"He that seeth me seeth Him that sent me."

Whether we speak of you or me, we are speaking of divine Life, individually expressing itself in all its harmony and perfection. This Life is Mind, and the faculties of Mind are universally and impartially expressed as all of Mind's ideas. Its faculties are never dependent on material conditions, or circumstances of birth, age or maturity. So let us learn to drop the "my" life, "my" vision, "my" understanding, "my" supply, and think in terms of Life, Vision, Understanding and Supply—and all of these individually expressed as you and me. Intelligence, wisdom, vision, power, are not personal, but are impersonal, impartial and universal.

In a universe governed by divine Principle, we never leave our state of peace, harmony, health and security. The law of Spirit, divine Principle, maintains our rightful place and condition of being. There are no material states or stages of consciousness, for there is but one Consciousness—spiritual Consciousness—in which there is neither matter nor material beliefs.

This is our only consciousness; there is no material substance, no material body, and in this consciousness we are found spiritual, incorporeal, harmonious and complete.

Health, harmony, wholeness are the direct result of consciousness. They are not dependent on mental manipulation, but on our consciousness of the harmony, peace and freedom of all God's universe. As we perceive that the Principle of Life can express Itself only harmoniously, completely and impartially, it is so unto us and we bring it into our human experience.

Errors are but shadows of belief thrown out by human thought onto the screen of visible form. There is in reality no error. Error has no substance, no body, no form, no law to enforce it, no mind to create it, express or respond to it. Error has no channel for its transmission. It has no existence apart from the false belief that is at the moment sustaining it. If our thought continues permeated with truths from the Bible or inspired metaphysical writings, these truths will take the place formerly occupied by false beliefs. The revelation of the perfect man will come about in a natural way, "not by might, nor by power, but by my Spirit," and we may rest assured that "the words that I speak unto you, they are Spirit and they are Life." The very thoughts that keep coming to us, these constitute the Word. Thus we should continue to know that all activity is not personal, but impersonal, universal and impartial, and that the activity of good, God, is infinitely expressed as us, as it is as every divine idea.

We learn to devote some part of every day to communion with God. While striving to obey the scriptural injunction to "pray without ceasing," we find it helpful to set aside specific moments in which to silently receive the influx of divine ideas, God's thoughts. Before retiring at night, it is well to have a sufficient time of quiet in which to realize a great sense of peace. In these moments we seek the assurance of God's presence, of our oneness, and a sense of spiritual freedom.

For thus said the Lord God, the Holy One of Israel; In returning and rest shall ye be saved; in quietness and in confidence shall be your strength.

Isaiah

Seek ye first the Kingdom of God, and His righteousness; and all these things shall be added unto you.

Jesus

This may seem to be one of the most difficult statements to understand or demonstrate until we know what the Kingdom of God is and how to seek it. The Kingdom of God is that state of consciousness wherein all is peace and harmony— therefore, when we have attained a sense of peace and harmony, we may know that we are in the Kingdom of Heaven, and that all things are being added unto us: health, wealth, activity, business, wholeness, holiness, freedom, joy and eternal bliss. When we retire at night with a complete feeling of His presence, then our rest cannot be invaded.

If we begin each new day with a short period of quiet in which to feel God's love permeating us, God's spirit empowering us, we can know that throughout the day His thoughts will be expressed through us since "He declareth unto man what are his thoughts." We can know that we will utter only His words, which are words of Truth and power, hearing only what His ear hears, because His presence shuts out mortal hearing and believing. We will understand and know with His Mind if we acknowledge that God is the only Mind, receiving and responding only to all things good. Realizing that His presence is power, we will know that every detail of our lives, every judgment, every action, every thought and move we make throughout the day will be of Him, manifesting as us. We will then see that there is no selfhood apart from God.

In pondering the statement "I am the Truth," it is clear that Jesus was not referring to his body or his brain, but his consciousness. Then the statement means, "My consciousness is the Truth." If Truth is that which makes free, is all power, then my consciousness is Truth, the power that makes free, the healer. Then I do not have to direct my consciousness or instruct it with affirmations or denials. I have to recognize that consciousness—the embodiment of every activity, element and substance of God—is who directs our ways, governs, guides and is also the God "who healeth all our diseases" and leads us.

Then it is my consciousness that embodies all the Truth there is, all the healing agency, all the right activity, all the Christ. Therefore, my consciousness—the universal Consciousness which is my consciousness—is the Truth, and the Life and the Way, and the bread, and the wine, and the water. The Kingdom of God is within me; not far off in some vague divine Mind or divine Consciousness, but in the DIVINE MIND OR CONSCIOUSNESS WHICH IS YOUR MIND AND CONSCIOUSNESS AND MY MIND AND CONSCIOUSNESS. This understanding removes the mystery and the miracle.

It must be clear to you that there is but one Mind or Consciousness and that this Mind and Consciousness is that of the individual. Therefore, the divine presence and power which meets every need for you is within you. It is your consciousness. The power and presence of God is not something that is outside of you, which must be contacted or prayed to. Your own consciousness, which is the universal, divine Consciousness, embodies within itself ALL presence, ALL power, ALL Principle, ALL law and ALL substance. Then your consciousness, everpresent and infinite, is the divine law unto your experience of health, harmony, home, position and supply. The consciousness of the individual has within itself ALL the presence and power of Life and Truth; therefore IT IS THE LIFE AND TRUTH.

Be alert! Do not attempt "mental work" in order to establish harmony, peace, justice. Human thought has no power to help you. Human thought is the troublemaker, not the healer. "The peace that passeth understanding" comes from the infinite divine power WITHIN YOU. Harmony is. Let it reveal itself to you from within. "Take no thought" regarding your so-called problems. LET divine ideas flow outward to you from the center of your being which is God. "Be still and know that I am God." "The Kingdom of God is within you," and in the sanctuary of your consciousness it reveals itself in all its glory. "Fear not, I am with you." Close your eyes and gently say "I," and you will find this to be literally true. There is no YOU separate and apart from God. "I AND MY FATHER ARE ONE."

The one thing you must keep in thought is this: "The Kingdom of God is within you." Never can you look to anyone or anything for what you seem to need, but as soon as a need becomes apparent, know that right then and there fulfillment exists as COMPLETED DEMONSTRATION within you. Within your very OWN CONSCIOUSNESS all good is embodied.

As you acquire the habit of looking within your own consciousness for the fulfillment of all needs, you will find that in a natural, normal way the fulfillment will appear. Do not look outside of yourself for peace, power, health or supply, but within your own consciousness, which is the Life, the Truth, and the Power.

## PART II

"ARISE, SHINE; for thy light is come." Thy light is recognized as here and now. "Lazarus [divine Being], come forth"—out of the tomb of human belief come into the light of the recognition of your divine life, here and now. Take off the "grave clothes" of superstition and of belief of mortal selfhood. "Loose him" from the bondage of fear and doubt, and set him free to realize and experience the freedom of Life, God —your life.

"One with God is a majority" and the Mind that was in Christ Jesus (my mind) calls *you* into the freedom of eternal Life here and now. "I say unto thee, arise," and as "I" call unto the divinity of your being, the shackles of sin, fear, disease and death fall to the ground—become nothingness.

"Cease ye from [being a] man, whose breath is in his nostrils" and be that which you are. "I and my Father are one"— you are not a mortal, nor a human being. "Thou shalt have no other Gods before me." Thou shalt recognize Spirit only as Creator, Father, and therefore the son, made in His image and likeness, as spiritual. "The life was the light of men" shows clearly that His life is the life of man, indestructible, indivisible, whole. His mind is the mind of man and so understands and expresses the truth of harmonious being.

Freedom from fear comes only with the recognition that the divine "I" is our only selfhood. We know that the divine "I" is God, and therefore I AM that which is invisible to mortal sense and that which is "hid with Christ in God." This "I" is self-possessed, self-maintained, self-sufficient and complete. It contains within itself all Life, all Love, all Being, and these forever harmoniously expressing themselves.

The "I" that I AM is the "Father within" and is "greater than he that is in the world," i.e., greater than any circumstance or condition. Recognizing this "I" to be the directing source of infinite good, we learn to depend more and more on the presence and power within "to prepare a place for us"— "to make the crooked places straight," and to make the "desert blossom as the rose." Never more shall we look outside the divine Self, the I AM. After all attention has been withdrawn from the manifested realm and placed on the I that I AM, then will we see God, good, even though we are yet in the flesh.

When a healthy man directs his feet to carry him in one direction, he does not find himself walking in the opposite direction. He knows that this is because he has dominion over his feet. He also knows that his body is not he, but the visible manifestation of him, the vehicle or form through which he expresses and moves himself. Is it not clear then that he, the individual, is invisible, incorporeal, and free from any so-called mental or physical condition? This *he* which seems to be a very personal and separate being is the impersonal, universal I AM individually expressing itself as you and as me.

Consciousness of the truth that this "I" that I AM is God is liberating because it enables us to perceive that: I AM not in bondage to physical organs or functions; that: I AM not subject to rents, bills, and debts; but that: I AM spiritually clothed, fed, housed, and therefore I AM without problems of health, home, intelligence or wealth.

Do you recall the astonishment of Moses when he realized "'I' AM THAT I AM"? This is why Isaiah could say, "My word . . . shall not return unto me void, but it shall accomplish that which 'I' please, and it shall prosper in the thing whereto 'I' sent it." Turning to Christ Jesus, we find these startling words: "He that seeth me, seeth Him that sent me," and "The words that I speak unto you, they are spirit and they are life."

At first glance many may believe that these inspired teachings refer only to the great men who uttered them. Many believe that these and other great leaders of religious thought have been divinely inspired, so that their words have greater weight or mightier power than others, but these words of Christ Jesus correct the fallacy: "He that believeth on me, the works that I do, shall he do also; and greater works than these shall he do."

Our most important need is the constant reminder of our true identity. Only as we live in the consciousness that " 'I and the Father are one" can we receive the continuous unfoldment of good. To be always alert to the truth that there is not God *and* man, because there is but *one* Life and *one* Mind. This Life and Mind which is God is your life and mind—so it cannot be two.

All discord and disease has its origin in the belief that we have a mind and life separate or apart from God. There is but one. We must remember that there is no law or power acting upon us—but that *we* are the law unto our body, business, home, supply. We have dominion over all that is in the sky, on the earth and under the water. We are the law unto it, whatever its name or nature. We exist as consciousness, embodying within ourselves every idea in the universe, and every idea is subject to and controlled by the consciousness in which it exists—and not "by taking thought" but through the unlabored energy of Mind, Life, forever expressing itself.

It follows that the allness of God, good, eliminates the possibility of evil in person, place, thing or circumstance, and any appearance of evil is but illusion. When the drunkard is awakened to the realization that his snakes exist only as illusion, he is healed, but as long as he thinks of them as something actual, he will want to get rid of them. Rid of what? Nothing—appearing as snakes. When we realize that all disease exists as illusion only, we are healed (and one heals others) because we no longer try to get rid of a condition which does not exist.

Our work is to live constantly in the consciousness that disease has no power. Our resistance to disease brings on the pain and even death. The disease of itself is powerless as we have proven in 70 years of metaphysical healing. The evil power is never in the disease or the condition itself, but always in the false concept of the condition. Keep uppermost in thought that no disease or other condition of itself has power for evil. All power, the only power, the ever-present power, is Life, Mind, Truth, ever expressing itself even where error seems to be.

Finally, the vital thing—gaining the spiritual sense of existence. It is simple to learn the letter when it is properly presented, but it takes practice and proof to gain the spiritual consciousness of Truth. We do not go quickly from material sense or the intellectual knowledge of Truth to spiritual realization.

Our whole work is growing out of mortal sense into immortal consciousness—and this entails "dying daily" to material beliefs; "being reborn" into spiritual sense; and all this through "praying without ceasing."

We should strive to become conscious of the abundant love and truth which is constantly unfolding from Mind—the Kingdom within. When we have fully realized that this Kingdom is within, that nothing can be added to or taken from the divine being which we are, we will more nearly live the Life of abundance—health, wealth, harmony and peace. This is our divine heritage. The joy of the revelation that we are now reflecting infinitely these divine attributes is ours when we realize that God has not created us; that He has manifested HIMSELF as us—that we are His own selfhood made manifest; that His Selfhood is the only Us there is.

God has and needs no channels. His selfhood is directly expressed as His creation. There is in heaven and on earth no one who needs healing, improving, enriching, employing, because God is and always has been our selfhood. Truth cannot be brought *to us*. The *belief* that we have needs is the reason we have to contend with problems.

"It is the Spirit that quickeneth"—the conscious awareness of Truth which reveals to us our true being. However, Spiritual Consciousness is God, and this is the consciousness of individual being, your own consciousness. It is not something separate or apart from you, something to be gained, earned, won or sought. There is but one consciousness and it embodies every quality of Love, every activity of Mind, ALL the harmony of divine Being. There is no selfhood apart from God; there is but one Life, one Being, one Mind. It is your life, your being, your mind.

Nothing can be added to you or taken from you, and into your consciousness nothing can enter that "defileth or maketh a lie." You are about your Father's business. Cause and effect being one, effect includes ALL that Cause is, here and now. Good does not flow from God to you, but it is inherent in Mind, and therefore in Mind manifest (you), for these are one.

Live every moment in the consciousness of your oneness with your divine Principle. "I and my Father are one"—not two. Rejoice in your oneness; that He is the life of your being and the joy of your heart. You are free because He is free. His freedom is your freedom; His life is your life; the harmony of His being is the harmony of your being; His immortality is the infinity of your life.

Give up the sense of personal possession. All that we possess of home, health, wealth, activity, intelligence, belongs to universal Mind, Life, Spirit, which we call God. These "possessions"—faculties and qualities of Mind—are expressed *as* the individual you and me, and therefore all that the Father hath and is, is expressed as the individual son. Within you and within me, within individual consciousness is perfection—perfect health, perfect body, mind, beauty, harmony, eternal being. This spiritual self was never born and can neither age nor die. It embraces within itself every requisite by right of this sonship as "joint-heir with Christ in God."

Only through spiritual sense are we able to discern our true identity as the Christ. Only through spiritual discernment are we able to pierce the veil of illusion and behold the spiritual universe here and now, perfect in its being. Exalted vision alone reveals: "Ye are the Light of the world."

# The Real Teacher

THE HUMAN MIND is not a teacher. It is not capable of teaching because it cannot convey Truth, since the Truth is not in it. The impartation of Truth from one individual to another is not the activity of the human mind. Some of the teaching in the field of metaphysics is nothing more than the transference of intellectually perceived truths from one so-called mind to another, because they who teach have not themselves advanced far enough in the understanding of Spirit and its activities. This accounts for the fewness of the students that are capable of healing. When Truth is properly taught, the student heals at once.

Divine Mind is the only Teacher, as the impartation of Truth is the activity of divine Mind. This action embodies the power of the Christ. Christ Jesus' teaching so imbued his disciples with the spirit of Love that they healed through the power of their own consciousness. It was healing without effort, or Christ healing.

This same healing gift is being bestowed on individuals today by the teachers who are living in the understanding of the Christ consciousness. However, it necessitates living the Christ. These teachers have forsaken ambition and have lost any desire they may have had to occupy positions of high temporal power. They have lost the personal sense of selfhood and have gained the impersonal Christ.

This reveals the true nature of teaching. Through no personal effort, or intellectuality, contact with them results in an uplifted state of consciousness in which Truth reveals itself to the student. From the "Mind which was also in Christ Jesus" come impartations of Truth to the student. Their source and power is directly from God, universal divine Mind.

Christ consciousness is that state of being which is ever aware of the Allness of good. It is "the Light in which there is no darkness"—no awareness of evil, of sin, disease, or of any other discord. This is an impersonal consciousness, although individually manifested by those who have realized the illusory nature of the personal self; those who have become conscious of the fact that they exist as the expression of the divine qualities, character and nature of God; that the personal selfhood materially and mentally can of itself "do nothing," whereas the image of God is the full reflection of His Being— of His infinity, eternality and immortality.

Christ is that state of consciousness which is man's Teacher. "All shall be taught of Me." This consciousness individualized in any age or nation will attract to it those humans to whom the urge has come to seek something higher than personal selfhood; seeking a higher good than matter or intellect can provide. These are the seekers for Truth, and they will ultimately find Truth wherever it is individualized—whether this individualization be a Moses, a Jesus, or anyone else sufficiently free of personal self as to have become an outlet for the revelation of true being.

"My sheep hear my voice"—certain it is that this quality in the mind and heart which urges one on in the quest for Truth enables us to recognize the individuality or individualized expression of Truth as the Shepherd or Teacher.

The Shepherd attracts "his own"—those "prepared for him from the beginning," prepared not for the person but for the Christ consciousness which he individualizes or represents.

The Teacher who accepts into his class (into his consciousness), for popularity or for gain, those not of his "sheepfold" will soon find himself lost in the maze of material beliefs, or laws of limitation. The personal self with its ambitions, inflated ego, must be put off in order that the unselfed, the impersonal Christ or Truth bear witness.

"Those that the Father giveth me shall come to me—and them I shall in no wise cast out." Those in whom I am established as Teacher (not a personal selfhood), those who recognize Christ, Truth, will come to me, and "I will receive my own."

# The Seven Steps

THERE ARE SEVEN foundational steps necesssary to the understanding of spiritual existence, and it is helpful to try to understand the Truth in the following statements:

1. "Call no man your father upon the earth; for one is your Father, which is in heaven."

When we catch even a small glimpse of this Truth, we start to see the meaning of preexistence and we can understand why it is that man was never born, and in fact that there never was a creation, but that all that is, is unfoldment within the Universal Consciousness, which is your individual consciousness.

2. "The earth is the Lord's and the fullness thereof."

By recognizing that everything that is, is a part of the Universal, is a possession of the Universal, and that everything that is in and of the Universal is forever expressing itself through the individual, we give up our sense of personal possession and start to draw from the Universal.

3. "The glory which I had with Thee before the world was" is still mine.

Here we recognize that there is no power apart from God, and therefore nothing has ever happened to separate us from the glory, power, dominion, purity, and spirituality that was ours in the beginning. In one step we wipe out the belief of material consciousness.

4. "Greater is he that is in you, than he that is in the world."

Now we are recognizing that Christ or the Word is greater than any condition or circumstance that may arise in the manifest world.

5. "I and my Father are one."

That is, my consciousness is the divine, infinite, eternal, Universal Consciousness individually expressed. Life is life, Mind is mind.

6. "He that is without sin among you, let him first cast a stone."

Only the consciousness that can see itself sinless, pure and perfect can see the harmony and wholeness of his neighbor, and under no circumstance must there be condemnation of self or another, because the Christ-Self, which is the only Self, must be seen as here and now.

7. "My grace is sufficient for thee."

Rest in the consciousness of divine perfection, universally and individually expressed. Rest in the consciousness that infinity and eternality and harmony of divine Being are forever expressing as man and the universe.

## FIRST STEP

THE FIRST STEP in the understanding of absolute Truth is revealed in the statement: "Call no man your father upon the earth; for one is your Father, which is in heaven." This reveals immediately the impossibility of there being a material body, once we have acknowledged Spirit alone as creator. This likewise eliminates mortal mind and all of its activities, character and nature, and all mortal existence that has beginning and ending, and leaves us with incorporeal spiritual man.

It is not sufficient to read these statements and agree with them, but it is necessary to make a specific application of them in all of the circumstances that arise in our human experience.

Actually God is not a creator but is Universal Consciousness, out of which all manifestation is evolved. Were there a creator, there would necessarily have to be a time of creation or beginning. Viewing Deity as Consciousness, the universal substance, and the universe as a manifestation or evolution of that spiritual substance enables us to see that individual life, evolved from universal Life, or the manifestation of infinite Life, was never created and can never end, but must forever remain as Life manifested, as divine Being individually formed, as eternal Consciousness individually expressed.

To know that "mortality is a myth" is to lose all fear of persons, circumstances or conditions. If a tree should seem to have snakes growing out instead of branches, we would not attempt either materially or mentally to remove the snakes. This would be foolishness, but we would stand still and know that this was an illusion and that as such it had no power to harm us in any way. With this sane viewpoint, the appearance of snakes would disappear and the branches of the tree become visible again.

Now actually this would not be a healing of snakes, nor would snakes actually disappear to make room for branches— an illusion would merely be dispelled.

Disease or lack represents snakes where branches are. In the very place where the discord or lack seems to be, there is pure spiritual Being, there is divine Life expressed.

The consciousness of the presence of Spirit eliminates the belief of matter; the consciousness of the presence of Christ dispels the illusion of mortal man; the consciousness of the omnipresence of divine Mind annihilates the belief of mortal mind and its activities and all its formations.

This represents the cornerstone of spiritual understanding.

## SECOND STEP

OUR SECOND STEP is: ''The earth is the Lord's and the fullness thereof.'' In the first step, we found it necessary to renounce human birth, mortal conception, earthly parentage —in order to realize that man is wholly spiritual, that not one trace of matter or human belief enters into the consciousness which is man.

It must follow that the source of man, infinite Spirit, must likewise be the possessor of all that is, in order to express this allness in and as what we know as creation or manifestation. ''Son, all that I have is thine'' involves first understanding that ''all'' belongs to universal Life. Then we can understand that universal Life can and does express *all* of its infinite qualities, nature and character individually as you and as me.

As there is no matter, all supply must be and IS spiritual. Home, furnishings, clothing, money, employment, business, etc.—all of these must be seen as spiritual ideas of Mind, *in* Mind, and then it can be appreciated how Mind can express these through *all* men, not just some men.

Give up the sense of personal possession. It is a wrong sense. All that you or I possess of health, wealth, home, activity, intelligence belongs to the infinite universal Mind, Life, Spirit, which we call God. These possessions, faculties, qualities of Mind are expressed as the individual you and me—and, therefore, *ALL* that the Father has and is, is expressed as the individual son. Within you and within me, within individual consciousness, is perfection—perfect health, perfect body, mind and spirit, perfect wealth, home, beauty and family. These are all embodied within our consciousness and go to make up our individuality.

In order to humanly enjoy these so-called earthly possessions, we need to realize that as "I can of mine own self *do* nothing," so I can of mine own self *possess* nothing, but *all* these are mine because all belongs to the universal source, and *all* are impartially, impersonally expressed in, through and as individual you and me. "The earth is the Lord's and the fullness thereof" and "Son, *all* that I have is thine" is the truth about spiritual supply and its earthly manifestation in individual experience.

Looking upon God as the infinite source, we look upon all men and things as manifestation. All having the same source, we need never look to any manifested being for anything, but for all things look directly to the SOURCE—or, better still, look within our own consciousness where infinite Mind is forever expressing its bounties.

## THIRD STEP

THE THIRD STEP is: "The glory which I had with Thee before the world was" is still mine. When we agree to "call no man father on earth," we naturally claim the divine Father-Mother God as our only parent, and thereby we claim for ourselves divine sonship. This spiritual self was never born and can neither age nor die. It embraces within itself every requisite by right of this sonship as "joint heir with Christ in God," thereby eliminating struggle, effort or striving for that which we naturally inherit.

Agreeing that "the earth is the Lord's and the fullness thereof," and that we are "joint heirs" to all of this infinite Kingdom, it becomes necessary only to *accept* our good, our health, our home or supply. All of these things are a part of the glory of God and became a part of our inheritance the moment we recognized our true parentage. Because God is omnipotence, there is no power to deprive us of any of the glory with which He has endowed us. We can, therefore, declare with emphasis, "All the glory I had with Thee in the beginning" is still mine. Remember that every divine idea is infinite; that every divine idea is omnipresent in Mind; and as there is but one Mind, whatever is a part of or present in this infinite Mind is in your mind and in my mind, and if *present* in Mind, it is evident as manifestation, because Mind and its manifestation are one—"I and my Father are one."

In practical application, wherever there seems to be a human need, know that then and there the fulfillment exists as omnipresent in Mind; that because there is only one Mind, it is present now in your mind and, therefore, manifested. It exists in Mind and manifests right where you are and NOW. You may claim it as your heritage; as part of that which Love imparted to you "in the beginning"; as part of the glory of the Babe, of the divine idea.

Nothing can ever be lost out of Mind; nothing can ever disappear from consciousness; and all must ever remain as part of that original glory, which is your consciousness.

## FOURTH STEP

THE FOURTH STEP is: "Greater is he that is in you, than he that is in the world." Here it becomes necessary to remember that Consciousness is God; that everything exists as an inseparable part of Consciousness; and also to remember that outside of Consciousness there is nothing. It naturally follows that Consciousness is greater than any of its formations; that Consciousness governs, controls, directs, leads, supports and sustains everything that is a component part of it, "from a blade of grass to a star."

In the Bible we learn that "the Kingdom of God is within you." This means that Consciousness is the very center of your being and FROM out of your consciousness emanates all of which you are conscious or aware. Out of Consciousness comes the universe in its entirety.

Does this mean that Consciousness controls your flesh and blood, or business, or automobile? Yes, indeed. Nothing can exist outside of Consciousness, or apart from its control. "I can of mine own self do nothing; the Father *within me*, He doeth the works."

Keep in mind the fact that invisible to human sense is the Power; the Father, divine Consciousness—and that this Consciousness is greater than anything in the material realm, or realm of manifestation.

This Consciousness constructs bodies and businesses; it governs all human contacts and relationships; it "goes before you to make the crooked places straight"; it "prepares a place for you"; it sets a table before you in the wilderness; it is your protector, supplier, as well as your protection and your supply.

## FIFTH STEP

THE FIFTH STEP is: "I and my Father are one"—that is, my individual consciousness is one with the divine, infinite, eternal Consciousness, but it is individually expressed as me. *Life* is life; *Mind* is mind; *Supply* is supply; etc.

Instead of declaring Truth, affirming Truth, stating Truth, we are to LET Truth declare itself to us, in us, through us and as us. Then are we really in unity, at-one, with this Mind or infinite Consciousness. To believe that affirming many quotations from the Bible or metaphysical writings is uttering the Word of God is folly. To believe that talking Truth, quoting truths, treating with Truth is wisdom or divine is absurd. This would lead to the belief that the best memorizer, or the best reader, or the most forceful speaker would be the best healer, which of course is not so.

The good LISTENER is the best minister of the Christ. We must "listen for the still small voice." We must let divine Mind unfold its truth to us; we must let Universal Consciousness reveal its infinite nature, character, qualities and plan to individual consciousness. Then we can truly say: "I and my Father are one." The impartation of Truth must be FROM Mind to us, and not from us to Mind, or even from us to another individual. "Mind spake" and it was so. God said: "Let there be light, and there was light."

Consciousness reveals and unfolds its beauties, harmonies and delights to individuals who are receptive and responsive. Mind selects the channels, persons or books, song or sermon, through which its truths are revealed to human consciousness —"You have not chosen me, but I have chosen you."

## SIXTH STEP

OUR SIXTH STEP is: "He that is without sin among you, let him first cast a stone." Only the consciousness that can see itself sinless, pure and perfect is realizing that there is but *one* consciousness and, therefore, only he can truly see the harmony and wholeness of his neighbor.

To live scientifically is to be conscious of but one Mind, one infinite, eternal Consciousness, impersonally and impartially manifested as all men. In this Mind there is neither sin nor disease, neither fear nor limitation—and, therefore, these negative qualities cannot be expressed by man.

The appearance of evil in ourselves or in others must always be met with the understanding that these qualities are not a constituted part of God and, therefore, are not inherent in God's image and likeness. This true knowing removes even the appearance of error.

Qualities of thought unlike the Divine cannot operate in human consciousness to cause disease or perpetuate it.

We must continually rise above the personal sense of man to find the perfection of Mind and its idea, of Love and its expression, of Life and its manifestation. We must not accept as true the varied appearances of evil, but look behind the manifested realm to the Manifestor, in order to rightly judge the manifestation—its qualities, nature and character.

Only through spiritual sense are we able to discern the real man that ever stands behind the mortal. Only through spiritual discernment are we able to pierce the veil of matter and behold the spiritual universe, here and now, eternal in its being.

Man is not mortal; he is immortal. Man is not composed of brain and flesh and bones, but of infinite qualities of good, individually expressed. Man neither sins nor dies, because man is God manifested, Life expressed, Love reflected, intelligence unfolded. This true view of man reforms the sinner and heals the sick. It is the "peace be still" to error of every name or nature.

Only a mortal could "cast a stone," could judge, criticize or condemn. God's man can never do these things. "The Mind that was also in Christ Jesus" neither judges nor condemns, and this holy Mind is man's only mind. All else is not Mind, but illusion; is not intelligence, but is belief; and therefore is without power or presence. There is but one Mind, and in this Mind is neither sin or punishment, neither judge nor judgment; and this Mind is the mind of man.

## SEVENTH STEP

Our seventh step is: "My grace is sufficient for thee." Moses failed to enter the "Promised Land"—the ultimate heaven or harmony—because he saw error as a lesser power with which God had to contend, instead of knowing error to be nothing, unknown to God. Our only duty is to know that God's work is done. Jesus knew that God is the only power, that there is no other power to oppose the infinite activity of God, good.

The dawning of the Christ confers a state of consciousness that is a state of grace. A state of grace is a state of consciousness which, recognizing that divine Love does not have to be used as a greater power to destroy a lesser power, knows that no lesser power exists. God is the only power. It is a state of consciousness that needs no denying of error. It is the perfect state of consciousness.

The purer the state of consciousness, the nearer we are to a state of grace, and the more clearly will the Christ operate in consciousness.

We all are states of consciousness, not persons. Jesus was a state of consciousness and was so thoroughly touched by the divine that he could detect error and dissolve it, which resulted in healing. This is a state of grace.

The affirmative state of consciousness is one that establishes at-one-ment with God without mental effort. This is a state of grace.

Remember it is the dawning of the Christ in consciousness that confers the state of grace, and this state of consciousness is sufficient for all needs.

# Truth

*The law was given by Moses, but*
*grace and truth came by Jesus Christ.*
                              —John 1:17.

UNDER PHARAOH the Hebrews had been in complete
and utter slavery, not only economically, but culturally as
well. They had not been permitted religious freedom, educa-
tional freedom, or cultural freedom any more than financial
freedom. Consequently they were at about the lowest level of
humanhood imaginable.

It was in this state that Moses found them, and wishing
to free them from their bondage, he took them out from under
Pharaoh and led them out into the desert. Unaccustomed as
they were to such freedom, they mistook liberty for license.
They became very unruly and difficult to manage, so that it
became necessary for Moses to set up many human codes—
codes of human conduct. One set of these codes we know as
the Ten Commandments.

One of the mistaken beliefs of many people in the religious world is that the Ten Commandments are spiritual commands, having to do with spiritual or religious life. This is not true. The Ten Commandments, with the exception of the First Commandment, constitute a code of human conduct. It is certain that to one of spiritual vision you would never have to say, "Thou shalt not steal," or "Honor thy father and thy mother." And it would be just as fantastic to tell them not to commit adultery; not to commit murder; not to covet or envy.

The Ten Commandments, then, do constitute law, and so now, as with Moses and the Hebrews in that intermediary stage of humanhood, it becomes necessary to have such a code of laws—of human laws—in order to teach men how to be just ordinary good humans. In the teachings of Christ Jesus you do not find any such commands about being *humanly* good. You are told, rather, that "My kingdom is not of this world." You are lifted into a spiritual atmosphere in which there is not even a thought or a temptation of being *humanly* bad. That is why we are told, "The law was given by Moses, but grace and truth came by Jesus Christ."

It is a very strange thing that now, nearly four thousand years since Moses gave the Ten Commandments, there still seems to be the necessity in the business world for groups such as the Kiwanis, the Lions and the Rotary that primarily affirm to the business world that "honesty is the best policy"; that we should live and work in honesty and cooperation with each other. True that we should, but you would think that during all of these four thousand years, the world would have outgrown the need for being admonished by businessmen to be honest, to cooperate, and not to compete to the extent of extinction.

In that sense, all of these organizations I have mentioned,

and others like them, are serving a wonderful purpose. The only strange thing about the situation is that there should be a need for such organizations; that in these four thousand years in which we have had the Ten Commandments, men have not yet learned to obey them without having a Club or a Police Department to tell them how to conduct themselves as good humans. *"Did not Moses give you the law, and yet none of you keepeth the law?"* John 7:19.

In my book *Spiritual Interpretation of Scripture* this is brought out—that Moses and his work with the Hebrews was entirely in the line of making better humans of them and improving their conditions on the human plane; although in doing this he also gave them a freer sense of religion, and he led them out into some degree of education. He brought out better conduct and made better humans of them, even though it was not permanent. We find in the Bible how many times the Hebrews kept sliding back into slavery, kept sliding back into their old evil ways. Then along would come another prophet or leader and bring them back into better humanhood.

Now, our modern world—and it is true all over the world —has been going through a similar experience as that of the Hebrews under Moses. Take, for instance, the great spiritual light given to the world by Jesus; yet, after a few hundred years, we see the world sink back into the darkness of the Middle Ages. Then we see the Western mystics, the movements that resulted in Eckhardt, Tauler, Fox, and the Quaker movement, and the great spiritual revival that came. But yet again watch the world go downhill into another age of darkness, and on until we come up to this present age.

It is not usually recognized, but in our own country we had much more spiritual light than would ordinarily be gathered from school study and from history. The men who framed

the Constitution, the men who went through the Revolution-
ary War and then finally formed this government, were men
not only of great human vision, but of spiritual vision as well.
They had a wonderful sense of freedom; a wonderful sense of
the value of liberty and of the individual Soul. If you will
closely observe the form of government which they set up,
you will find that the individual was paramount—the individual was given great significance.

So, in this present time, we find that this institution which
they set up of human good, based on spiritual values, has led
this country forward into great prosperity. Then, through circumstances or individuals or tides or currents, all of a sudden
that particular form of human institution is ridiculed and is
almost wiped out. No, not quite, but very nearly. If it is wiped
out with these trends that we are meeting today in the business and political world—if it is wiped out—there will be
another period of darkness and many hundreds of years before
the light again comes, revealing the importance and the integrity of individual consciousness. But in this again we see the
ceaseless movement of humanhood, even of good humanhood,
that even after it is achieved, a crash, a man, an event, can
come and carry it down. That is the picture of humanhood.
No matter how bright it is; no matter how good it is; no matter
how clever it is; it reaches a certain level and then fails.

With such examples as these before us, we as individuals
must begin to look out on the world, with all of its human
good, human cleverness, human ingenuity mounting up, and
ask ourselves, "What is it for? Where is it going, and why?
What is it all about? Supposing I do get to be a millionaire, or
supposing I do get to be the head of an industry, then what?"

The answer is in this illumination: No *human* achievement is worthwhile, and no *human* accomplishment is perma-

nent, unless it is imbued with the Spirit. No matter how much human ingenuity one has, no matter how much human intelligence or physical strength, it will all still eventually end up on the rock pile of the world, unless one attains a measure of the Spirit, of the Mind that was in Christ Jesus. That is what we call the SPIRITUAL LIFE.

This, then, must be the aim of all our metaphysical work. It must have as its basis the development, the cultivation and the unfoldment of a SPIRITUAL LIFE, illumining our whole world, our body, our business, our being. That is the basis for this work, as we know it in this particular avenue or approach to Life, and which you will gather in the study of *The Infinite Way.*

You know, one of the saddest things we encounter in this work is the number of metaphysical students who are *using* Truth to make the demonstration of a parking space, or a new automobile, or a house to live in, or something of the kind. That is the tragedy that has sprung up in the metaphysical field—of individuals, many times a great percentage of the followers, who look on God as just a *means* of getting a better job, of earning ten or a hundred dollars a week more, of finding a better place to live, of getting a wife—or getting rid of one; of getting a husband—or getting rid of one. Now, unless one begins to see that God is not to be used merely for the attainment of some greater degree of material good, then one has not the vision at all with which to approach the SPIRITUAL LIFE. True, in the end, the result of our work is the attaining of success, of health, of a perfect body, of a perfect business, of a perfect home, but the difference in the approach is in the motive and the manner.

In our work, we take the pattern given us by Jesus in Luke 12:22–32, where he tells us to "Take no thought for your life,

what ye shall eat; neither for the body, what ye shall put on.
. . . Consider the ravens: for they neither sow nor reap . . .
and God feedeth them," and "Consider the lilies how they
grow: they toil not, they spin not; and yet I say unto you, that
Solomon in all his glory was not arrayed like one of these."
Then he reminds us that "the nations of the world" take
thought for the things they shall eat and drink—they are concerned with making demonstrations. But Jesus says, "Your
Father knoweth that ye have need of these things" and to
"Rather seek *ye* the kingdom of God; and all these *things*
shall be added unto you. . . . for it is your Father's good pleasure to give you the kingdom."

Now, in this work, in this approach of ours, the goal is
SUCCESS; the goal is success and harmony even in what the
human world calls peace, joy, abundance. In other words, it
is the attainment of security, the attainment of health, the
attainment of a happy home. It is true that is the goal, but
the manner of achieving it is by "taking no thought" for these
things; by dropping them from thought and beginning with
God—with the recognition of the *presence* of God and the
acknowledgment of the *power* of God.

Then, we can see that our approach to SPIRITUAL LIVING
must begin with the recognition of our ONE-NESS with God.
And, as our approach begins, even so must our very days begin
and our noons and our nights and our sleeping periods. Each
one of these must begin with the recognition of the *presence*
and *power* of God and of our Oneness with Him. In the chapter
entitled "Meditation" of my book *The Infinite Way* I have
outlined all of this for its readers and students, pointing out
the importance at the moment of awakening in the morning,
before getting out of bed, of the first thought being GOD,
omnipresent God; and individual Oneness, my individual

Oneness with God; the recognition that the place whereon
I stand is holy ground. Why? Because "I and the Father are
one." Then, where I am, God is. Therefore, both the Father
and I are standing here, and that makes it holy ground.

"I and the Father are one." Then, there is not God *and*
me, there is not God *and* you, but only ONE, and that One
is God. "Thou seest me, thou seest the Father which sent
me . . . for I and the Father are one."

Now, that is the Way, as we teach it in this approach.
Our very first thought in the morning is GOD. Not, "Where
shall I go today to make a sale?" or "What shall I do to bring
out a clever ad?" But a recognition and a realization of OMNI-
PRESENCE and of ONENESS. These are two great words:
"Omnipresence" and "Oneness."

When we have established in consciousness the realization
of our Oneness with God, we can then go about our physical
preparations for the day. We can bathe, shave, eat and get
ready, but we still have no right to leave our homes without
sitting quietly for a minute or two and again realizing the
Presence. If we don't sit down, we can at least be conscious
of this realization while we are walking around. Let us realize
this Presence that goes before us to make the crooked places
straight; that walks beside us; that remains behind to bless
all those who pass that way. Then, wherever we go, It is there
to meet us, and wherever we leave, It remains behind as a
blessing to others. That is making It universal, isn't it? That
is recognizing that this great Presence and Power is not something for us alone. (Heaven help the world if any individual
could utilize it for his own good, so as to leave the rest of the
world out!)

There, too, is where so many people on the Path miss their
goal and wonder why their demonstrations are not made. They

think there is a possibility of God or Truth or Spirit doing something for them that does not, at the same time, include the Universal good. You know, it would be as impossible for one to gain a benefit that did not accrue to everyone as it would be for the sun to shine and just light up your particular garden, or mine, and leave the rest of the world out in the cold.

God is Universal. God is Universal Good. God is Universal Omnipresence. But if you and I do not *consciously* know that, if we do not *consciously* realize it, it is as if it were not true. It is as though there were a million dollars in the bank in our name that we did not know about and we spent our life in lack. Therefore, each of us must make this universality of God, of Good, of Omnipresence a part of our daily consciousness. We cannot demonstrate more than we can be conscious of, because all demonstration lies in the realm of consciousness.

Now, if you can open your consciousness to the fact that God is Universal Good, that God is Universal Law, that God is a Universal Principle, and therefore in governing, maintaining and sustaining you It is doing the same to all with whom you come in contact, It is doing the same for all those with whom you become associated, then you have brought the universality of God to bear on your experience.

You will find that if you ever earn one dollar through spiritual means, through spiritual realization, your economic security will be assured for the rest of your life. You will not have to make the demonstration over again. Why? Because the realization of a spiritual Truth that resulted in the activity of God being made manifest as supply today must be a continuing experience, since the activity of God, once realized, is a permanent dispensation.

It would seem that you have to go out every day to sell goods, or win your law cases, or you have to sit at home and design new houses, but that is all a picture that goes on in the outer world. Once individual consciousness has become activated by this divine Principle; once you have made yourself consciously One with God and have felt that contact; once you have realized what the name and nature of God is, where it is and how it operates; from that time on, you will never have to think about economic security, or how to get money, or how to get success. Your whole mind will be just on your job, doing it. The result will always take care of itself. Our great experience is in arriving at the very first demonstration of this.

It is easy to teach men how to sell. It is easy to teach men how to be accountants or insurance men. Given a man of ordinary intelligence, there is no great difficulty about it. The difficult thing is to bring an individual to the place where God is a Reality in his consciousness, not merely a word or a statement or a phrase.

Spiritual Truth may be read over and over, or recited again and again, but it will do nothing for you until there is some measure of *realization* with it. We all, on this Path, have those experiences where some particular statement of Truth will stand out and register with us above others; that when we read it or remember it, it is almost as though we touch it within our own being. It becomes "meat and drink" to us. Why? Because it is a *realized* Truth. It has become *real* to us. It may only be a grain of Truth, but a grain of Truth *realized* is enough to carry any man through life.

When you do find a statement of Truth that becomes realization to you, or when you actually *realize* anything that has to do with Truth and you can *touch* it within your own consciousness so that it becomes reality to you, from then on you are in Heaven, and every step taken is just a forward one, onward and upward. There, though, is the all-important part: finding a statement of Truth, or the realization of Truth, or an approach of Truth that *registers* spiritually with you; that you touch in your heart and your Soul and your Mind.

We must see and understand that the intellectual perception of Truth is not spiritual *awareness*. Look how many statements of Truth the student knows; how many statements of Truth he declares and then says, "Well, why doesn't it work? I have declared this a hundred times today and it hasn't done a thing for me." Or, "I have recited the Lord's Prayer and made my affirmations and denials a thousand times, and it just isn't doing anything for me. I wonder if I am different than other people?"

Yes. In this degree: The intellectual statement or perception of Truth is not spiritual *awareness*. They are two entirely different things. It is true that the intellectual awareness may be a first step (I think that it usually is, as most people have an intellectual awareness of Truth before they catch the Spirit, although some few have the Spirit of Truth long before they know what Truth is). However, it does not make any difference which way this Spirit of Truth comes; the main thing is that it must come.

From our standpoint, the approach to this spiritual awareness of Truth begins with the conscious effort of filling our consciousness with the idea of God's presence, God's allness, God's omniscience immediately on awakening in the morning, and then throughout the day continuing in that Word. "Thou wilt keep him in perfect peace whose mind is stayed on Thee." And don't ever fool yourself: "stayed" is an important word in that quotation. "Stayed on Thee." It can't just be five or ten minutes' work in the morning and then a forgetting of God until the next morning. There has to be some kind of a process, some kind of a realization within one, that makes it possible to make God a *continuing experience.*

Now, that might sound as if it were a very difficult task. It isn't at all, because every time we go out of our home, or the office, it can't be too difficult to just smile, and in that smile to realize, "Thank you, Father, I know You are here with me." It can't be too difficult, if you have a business appointment, to train yourself to stop for a little while and realize: "Well, you know that fellow I am going to meet? Why, God is his Mind as well as mine, and all I can meet there is intelligence and love, and all that he can meet here is intelligence and love."

Of course, when you take that attitude, you must be prepared if he does not want to buy what you have to offer, because that very realization of yours may save him from wanting what he does not need. But be willing, be willing.

There, too, this same attitude must apply in our driving. How often do we, in this Truth work, realize that God is *my* driver, God is *my* intelligence, and then we start worrying about the other fellow: what kind of a driver he is, as if God were not the Universal Mind and, therefore, the Mind of that other individual too.

And so we begin, all through the day to realize God as Universal Love, Universal Intelligence, Universal Mind, and gradually we begin to see God in every individual we meet. Even if at first he humanly does not measure up to it, we will have to look right behind the eye and say, "My fellow, no matter what you think you are outwardly, behind those eyes is the very presence of God." That, too, is the recognition of God in a universal way.

There are so many opportunities of reminding ourselves of the presence of God. Whenever we sit down to eat, whether it is for breakfast, luncheon, dinner, or for that little cup of coffee in between, we are missing the mark unless we again inwardly smile and say, "Thank you, Father," recognizing God as the Source. Yes, it might be that your pocketbook or your business appears to be the channel or avenue, but it is only through the recognition of God as the source of your business, as the source of your supply, as the source of your very existence that your supply, as well as your existence, becomes an absolute permanent and infinite thing. Only as we gain spiritual vision, recognizing God as the Source, is success an absolute spiritual surety.

You will notice that I use the word "God" in referring to Source. Many people might be offended at the use of the word "God" in this manner. That is all right, too. There is no harm done for them not to like it, as you cannot like it unless you have an actual *feel* of what it means. For those who feel that they cannot use the word "God" in this connection, there are many synonyms: Truth, Spirit, Soul, Principle, Mind, Substance, Intelligence, and many others that are now, in metaphysical language, so universally understood. Some people understand God as Mind. Some people really thrill to the understanding of "the Christ"—they *feel* that term, "the Christ." With others, it might leave them cold, but to know God as Principle means a great deal to them.

It really does not make any difference what *name* you give to God, because none of them would be correct. That is one thing we know. Our friend, Lao-tzu, told us that many, many years ago when he said that the God that can be named cannot be the infinite God. So, if you can name It, that cannot be IT. God does not come within range of our *human* awareness or finite senses. When God is *realized*, it is never with a name. Those who have *realized* God would not know how to describe the experience.

However, for our purpose we may use any name that suits

our particular state of consciousness or state of development. The main thing is to find a name, or to find a realization that will fit into our daily affairs. Now, all of this comes under the heading of spiritualizing thought—in other words, the conscious effort to stop living in the material sense of things, and to so spiritualize thought that everything we touch takes on some kind of spiritual sense for us.

I said this to a friend recently, that the reason for much of the world's economic discord, is the belief that supply is material. The Marxian doctrine is based entirely upon the material concept—the concept that everything is matter. All Socialism, or Communism, is based on this material doctrine: there is just so much for so many, and they set about getting it divided up.

Capitalism, on the other hand, is not material at all. Surprising as that may seem to people, Capitalism is based entirely on *spiritual values*. A very good example of this is one which you have probably heard many times—of the man who went to J. P. Morgan and wanted to borrow a million dollars. He told Mr. Morgan that he was tied up in so many different ways that he did not have the collateral to put up for the loan.

Mr. Morgan looked at him and said, "Collateral? Certainly, you have collateral. Haven't I known you for ten years? I wouldn't want any better collateral than your character." That is Capitalism in operation. Capitalism is based on credit, and credit is based on character, on integrity, on *spiritual values*. There is not as much actual money in all the world as is used right in one of our large cities. Have you ever stopped to think of that? There isn't that much money in all of the world. You might ask, "How can that be?" Only through Capitalism in operation: credit on the value of character and integrity and all of these things that we have built up, which entitle us to receive actual merchandise for which we do not immediately pay.

In this work, we go a step higher in our Capitalism, because we find our actual capital to be not merely *our* integrity, but we have come to the place of realization of which Jesus spoke when he said, "I can of mine own self do nothing"—"My doctrine is not mine, but His that sent me." We know that it is the *integrity* of God which is the character of our individual being; that we are not manifesting *human* honesty, or *human* integrity; but what we are doing is setting aside our human desire for anything and everything and showing forth the glory of God. That is SPIRITUAL LIVING; that is the teaching of all Truth. We have no integrity of our own, no honesty, no loyalty, no healing power. Everything there is, is of the Father. That is the Principle we are showing forth.

When we arrive at that realization, we have *spiritual* Capitalism; we have a Capitalism that is absolutely infinite and eternal and omnipresent. But as far as the world is concerned, that has not yet been touched. It rests today with the metaphysicians of the world to really show that this type of living is *profitable* and is *practical*.

You know, that is the first thing the world tells us: "What he is teaching isn't practical." I remember that during the last war, I wrote on that saying of Jesus: "They that take the sword shall perish with the sword." They said to me then, "That isn't practical. You can't do that in these days. It was all right in Jesus' day, but not today." They forgot that war was more universal in the days of Jesus than it is today.

Yes, in all times the world that is limited by its own concepts will tell you that *this* is not practical. But it IS practical. It is so practical that no matter where an individual finds himself this minute, if he actually follows a program of *spiri-*

*tualizing thought*, of holding thought steadfastly to God throughout the day (and that is the key)—next year he will be well on the way of showing forth peace and harmony and success. That is the secret of making a success of our existence; not just making a continual round of demonstrations.

The sooner you make an actual *contact*, that is, have the actual *feel* of Truth, the sooner you will be on the real spiritual Path, and that is when your real advance begins. Do not be content with just the mumbling of statements of Truth. Making statements of Truth is the first step for most of us. It is an approach. An affirmation here or a denial there; all of that is an approach, but do not be stopped there. Remember, it is far better to have one page or one quotation—just one quotation— that actually *registers* within us than it is to know the whole Bible from Genesis to Revelation.

So our work should be: Let our first thought in the morning be a conscious awareness of the presence of God, carry it with us throughout the day, and when retiring at night. Live in the *conscious awareness* of God, and let that unfold and carry us where it will.

# The Secret of the Twenty-Third Psalm

## MEDITATION ON PRAYER

IT IS THROUGH our understanding of prayer that we are able to bring the activity of the Kingdom of God, Harmony, Wholeness, into our individual experience.

If prayer, as it is generally understood, were really prayer, the world would be free of sin, disease, death, wars, famine, drought . . . all of these things would have disappeared from the earth in the thousands of years that the subject of prayer has been taught. Scripture tells us that if we pray and do not receive an answer, it is because we have been praying amiss and, if we judge by that, the world has been praying amiss for some thousands of years. The question is whether or not we know any more about prayer now.

Our progress in developing a clearer understanding of prayer has been rather slow, and up to the present time it is primarily an advance in the understanding of prayer as it touches upon our individual problems. The great problem of bringing peace on earth . . . good will to men . . . is still not solved.

So it becomes our work to devote as much time as possible to the study of the subject of prayer . . . to meditation upon that subject . . . until we come into higher and higher concepts of prayer.

We will know whether or not we are doing that by the results in our experience. If we are touching a higher note in prayer, we will have better health, better wealth . . . more of it . . . and a greater degree of harmony in all of our experience.

All too often, prayer consists, to too great a degree, of words, statements, quotations . . . whereas prayer, itself, actually is wordless. Prayer has NOTHING to do with anything that we voice . . . whether in the form of a petition, affirmation, denial or any other form of speech or thought. Rather, prayer is that which we become aware of IN THE SILENCE . . . the Word of God uttering Itself within our consciousness.

In other words, we do not pray unless prayer can be understood as a STATE of RECEPTIVITY. Actually, the Word of God is nothing that WE say but, rather, that which God says WITHIN US.

One form of meditation is to quietly consider some idea concerning God . . . think upon it or even voice it . . . but dwell upon it for only a short time. Then, become receptive and LET the meditation come through from God.

In other words, God does the meditating . . . we become aware of the fruits of that meditation.

In an introduction to an old edition of the Bible, we read:

"For is the Kingdom of God become words or syllables? Why should we be in bondage to them if we be free?"

IS the Kingdom of God words? IS the Kingdom of God syllables? NO! The Kingdom of God is WITHIN YOU . . . and that Kingdom of God must make Itself manifest to you. IT must declare Itself to you . . . utter Itself to you . . . voice Itself to you . . . and so, the Kingdom of God is not YOUR words nor YOUR syllables.

In our prayers, very often we carry around problems and we wonder what form of treatment we could use for this particular problem or that particular problem . . . or what form of prayer . . . or if there were some greater understanding we could acquire as to HOW to pray.

If you are having that experience, ponder this passage and the realization in it . . . "For IS the Kingdom of God become words or syllables?" . . . "WHY should we be in bondage to them [that is to the words or syllables] IF we be free?" Scripture teaches that we ARE free . . . we are children of God . . . if children, then heirs . . . if heirs, then joint heirs in Christ with God.

We are ALREADY free. If we were not free, there is no God power that could make us free.

We ARE free, and the entire truth teaching IS, of course, to bring out that realization or revelation of our present freedom . . . not to MAKE it so. It would be well for us to remember, with any of the problems now bothering us, that we might just as well NOT be in bondage to words or syllables or statements of truth but be willing to sit a while and let God reveal Its plan TO us . . . Its plan FOR us . . . TO us.

We find this in the Smith translation of the scriptures, the 19th Psalm: "The heavens are telling the glory of God . . . the sky shows forth the work of His hands. . . . Day unto day pours forth speech. . . . Night unto night declares knowledge. There is no speech nor are there words . . . their voice is not heard, yet their voice goes forth through all the earth and their words . . . to the ends of the world."

The last four lines go back to the first, "The Heavens are telling the glory of God." But then it says: "There is no speech nor are there words." And that is true. The heavens are not voicing themselves in words or speech and yet they ARE telling the glory of God.

"And the sky shows forth the work of His hands." And it says: "Their voice is not heard."

Certainly, the sky has no voice and yet it does show forth the work of His hands.

"Yet their voice goes forth," that is, the heavens and the sky and the day and the night . . . their voice goes forth without speech . . . without syllables . . . without words. Their voice goes forth and declares.

And so it is that our entire experience is one that shows forth the glory of God . . . it TELLS the glory of God. Our whole experience . . . our entire life . . . our bodies . . . are continuously showing forth the work of His hands.

If, at this moment, our bodies, our health, do not seem to be showing forth that divine harmony, it is ONLY because we have come under the belief that we have health of our own . . . bodies of our own . . . powers of our own . . . instead of realizing that ALL that concerns us in the body, in the purse or in the home is God showing Itself forth, manifesting Its beauties, Its nature and Its character.

The moment we make the transition from the belief that we HAVE health, that we can lose or gain . . . the moment that we give up the idea, the belief that we have health that can be improved, and understand that the only health that there is in all the universe is the health of God, manifesting itself as the health of our bodies or being . . . then do we come into the realization of this 19th Psalm: "The heavens are telling the glory of God," and they are doing it without words and without speech.

"The sky shows forth the work of His hands," and it does it without words and without speech.

"Day unto day pours forth speech." Yes, but day unto day does not talk. It only pours forth speech in the sense of pouring forth the harmony of God's being.

"Night unto night declares knowledge." And it does so without voicing it in speech or other impartation of ideas, except through the activity of showing off God's glory.

Now . . . ALL that we are and ALL that we hope to be is GOD showing Itself forth as our health . . . as our strength . . . as all of the good in our experience. Then, let us give up AT ONCE the belief that our health or wealth is dependent upon certain ARRANGEMENTS of words into treatments or prayers, for the Kingdom of God is NOT words or syllables . . . the Kingdom of God is already established within YOU.

Give up the belief that your health or your wealth or home can be dependent upon anything other than the activity of God. ONCE you have seen that point . . . that it is the activity of God that maintains the harmony of your being . . . you will commence to see a new light on the subject of prayer.

# PRACTICAL INTERPRETATION OF THE TWENTY-THIRD PSALM

CONSIDER THE 23rd Psalm. Here is a form of prayer that harmonizes most beautifully with the message of The Infinite Way and its idea of prayer.

"The Lord is my Shepherd, I shall not want." In that statement there is no APPEAL to God for anything . . . there is no TURNING to God for anything . . . there is not even an EXPECTANCY of GOOD from God. There IS a POSITIVE statement that "The Lord IS my Shepherd," and it naturally follows that "I shall not want."

Think upon that form of prayer. "The Lord is my Shepherd, I shall not want." There is no TURNING to God . . . no trying to reach God . . . no old-fashioned petition . . . not even the new-style affirmation. There is ONLY the recognition that since God IS and since God is MY Shepherd . . . my individual shepherd . . . guide . . . protector . . . guard . . . maintainer and sustainer . . . because this IS true, "I shall not want." There is no question at all. There is confidence . . . there is assurance . . . "I shall not want."

There is no seeking for supply . . . no attempt to demonstrate supply . . . only the calm, clear assurance, "I shall not want." Understand this . . . it is utterly impossible to want!

"He maketh me to lie down in green pastures, He leadeth me beside the still waters."

Again, there is no turning to God . . . not in any way, shape, manner or form. Not only does He PROVIDE green pastures but (notice this) "He MAKETH me to lie down" in them. It is not a matter of choice as to whether you WANT to lie down in green pastures or not . . . nor is it a matter of punishing you for your sins by keeping you out of the green pastures.

It is simply that "He MAKETH me to lie down in green pastures."

You should feel a sense of release as you realize that the burden is no longer on your shoulders, to govern yourself, maintain yourself, sustain yourself or even to find the right kind of prayer.

"The Lord is my Shepherd, I shall not want. He maketh me to lie down in green pastures, He leadeth me beside the still waters. He restoreth my soul. He leadeth me in the path of righteousness for His name's sake."

Observe, all the way through, there is no attempt to gain God's favor, no attempt to seek God's goodness, no attempt in any way to reach out for God . . . just this constant, confident assurance.

"Yea, though I walk through the valley of the shadow of death, I will fear no evil, for Thou art with me."

This is truly a miracle of prayer. As you have experienced periods of trial and tribulation . . . serious illness . . . family troubles . . . lack . . . limitation . . . loss of fortune . . . has it not seemed natural to feel that SOMEHOW you have become separated from God . . . in some manner you had slipped AWAY from God . . . for some reason God was not WITH you and thus, having lost contact, you must now get back to God. Now you can see the error of your thinking . . .

"Yea, though I walk through the valley of the shadow of death, I will fear no evil, FOR THOU ART WITH ME."

Even as he walks through the valley of the shadow of death, he cannot fear. Yet that is not true of us. We touch that valley of the shadow of death . . . or lack and limitation . . . or unemployment . . . or whatever the error may be . . . and we BEGIN to fear.

This fear begins for one reason only . . . lack of the full

realization that God is going through the valley of the shadow of death with us.

Behold, here, a whole new concept of prayer. We are not trying to GET God to be with us on this trek through the valley of the shadow of death. We are not reaching OUT for God. We are not even trying to have our fears stilled, since this recognition that God walks WITH us doesn't always save us FROM that walk through the valley of the shadow of death, but at least, if we are called upon to FACE the valley of the shadow of death, this statement tells us HE walks through it WITH us . . . "THOU ART WITH ME."

If you would just take that one statement and realize . . . what difference does it make WHAT the present valley of the shadow of death is . . . what difference does it make WHAT particular trial you are going through as long as you KNOW with all the confidence within you . . . that God is walking through the valley of the shadow of death WITH you . . . GOD is walking through this trial WITH you.

In *Spiritual Interpretation of Scripture* you will find the story of Joseph and his brethren . . . Joseph, the pampered and favorite son of his father, who probably expected to go through life very easily, quietly, calmly, with no trials or tribulations . . . and probably with no great victories . . . since he was the beneficiary of his father's great wealth and favoritism. However, it was not to be that way. Through the jealousy and deep malice of his brethren, Joseph was brought to the pit and thrown in, to be killed or sold into slavery (which was considered worse than death).

Finally, Joseph found himself in Egypt where he worked up from slavery to a responsible position in the household of the ruler. He has just about satisfied himself that now God is WITH him, when suddenly he is thrown into prison. He pleaded innocent but, innocent or not, he is in prison and, according to sense, AGAIN he is WITHOUT the presence of God as he is left there for several years. After he is freed, he rises, ultimately, to be the virtual ruler of Egypt.

Then the brethren came. They were the ones who had thrown him into the pit . . . sold him into slavery . . . brought about ALL his troubles. Now they came seeking a favor. They needed food and Joseph had it. Joseph gave it to them.

When the brethren attempt to apologize for their actions and express their sorrow, Joseph reflects the thoughts of David and says, "You did not do these things to me . . . God did them. God sent me, before you, into Egypt."

There is a high concept of prayer in that statement. There is a prayer worth remembering. It is not the devil . . . it is not mortal mind . . . it is not the opposite of God that brings about man's discords and diseases. It is God, Itself, that walks with man through his trials and temptations to bring him to some major victory, instead of leaving him alone to be just a healthy or wealthy human being, accomplishing nothing in his three-score years or more of life on this plane.

The average person accomplishes very little on earth except make a living and raise a family. As for any REAL contribution to showing forth the Glory of God, the average person has very little to show in that respect.

KNOW THIS . . . it is MEANT that we should bring forth spiritual fruitage . . . that we should show forth the handi-work of God . . . that we should show forth the Glory of God . . . but if we are going to rest on just our perfect health or perfect wealth, we are falling short of our true destiny.

Joseph recognized what YOU are going to recognize . . . that envy, jealousy, malice, hate, infection, contagion, depressions, changing governments, cannot bring discord or inharmony to you. Only GOD can bring you to a realization of your true identity in one way or another, and while you are going through the fiery furnace, while you are going through the forty years across the desert with Moses or while you are on the cross with Jesus (it does not make any difference what the nature of your trial or tribulation . . . they had every kind of them in scripture) at least you can know that GOD is there WITH you, walking through the experience also.

Had God not been with Jesus on the cross, there would have been no resurrection from the tomb and no ascension. Only the Power of God in the consciousness of Jesus could have brought about the resurrection.

Had there been NO God on that forty-year trek with Moses, there would have been no entrance to the Promised Land . . . there would have been no freedom for the Hebrews.

Had there been no God with Joseph, there would have been no mounting up from slavery to virtually being the ruler of the great country of Egypt . . . and great it was in that day.

Whatever the problem you are facing, try to realize this . . . you are NOT going through it alone . . . even though it is the valley of the shadow of death, you need fear no evil for GOD is with you. Consider that high concept of prayer . . .

"Thy rod and Thy staff they comfort me."

Whatever you are going through, there is a staff to lean upon and there is a rod to keep you in line. There IS some form of discipline. There IS some form of teaching. There IS some form of spiritual help to lean upon. You must KNOW this with all your knowing and then ACT with complete confidence in that KNOWING.

Elijah nearly forgot that when he was fed by the ravens and the widow and found cakes baked on the stones. He nearly forgot that it was the presence of GOD that provided those

things for him . . . NOTHING ELSE . . . and that they were
provided for him so that he, ALSO, might successfully walk
through the valley of the shadow of death and finally come to
that place where God reveals to him that he has saved out a
congregation of seven thousand of those who did not bow their
knees to Baal.

For YOU there is a congregation of seven thousand. For
YOU there is a SPIRITUAL mission . . . a SPIRITUAL purpose
on earth . . . and the PARTICULAR trial or tribulation through
which you may now be going (or a whole series of them, if
necessary) is for the sole purpose of leading you to your ultimate demonstration . . . something that could NOT have been
done without that PARTICULAR trial or tribulation.

This is the way of the cross . . . it is the way of the crown
. . . but notice that the crown comes long after the crucifixion.
First the crucifixions come (and many of them), and for that
reason the person entering the spiritual path MUST understand that "I come, not to bring peace but a sword . . . to
divide households," to break up EVERYTHING that would
give you ease and comfort in material circumstances and conditions.

There can be no spiritual progress until you have overcome
the world. As long as you are using Truth merely to increase
your human good . . . increase your weekly income . . . re-
model your home . . . acquire a better automobile . . . you
have not even TOUCHED the spiritual path.

In each case of the Hebrew prophets, you will notice that
their mission was NOT a personal one . . . their mission was
not just one of human good or just ADDING human good to
the world . . . it was ALWAYS a SPIRITUAL MISSION.

The same is true of you. YOU have a spiritual mission
whether, at this moment, you know it or not. EVERYONE

has a spiritual mission and EVERYONE, ultimately, will find it.

ONCE you have entered this spiritual path, there is no way to turn back. You may try it temporarily but you will be driven, forced back into this spiritual path since there IS this, "THOU ART WITH ME."

"Yea, though I walk through the valley of the shadow of death, I will fear no evil, for THOU art with me."

Then it is said, "Thou preparest a table before me in the presence of mine enemies. Thou anointest my head with oil. My cup runneth over."

Here, again, is simply the statement of that which IS. "Thou preparest a table." No affirmation to make it come true . . . no petition . . . no seeking God . . . merely a statement. This is high prayer.

"Thou preparest a table before me in the presence of mine enemies. Thou anointest my head with oil. My cup runneth over."

Then:

"SURELY goodness and mercy shall follow me ALL the days of my life!"

How confident he is, "SURELY goodness and mercy. . . ."

There is another important thought there also: ". . . ALL the days of my life."

Once you realize that God cannot operate today and not tomorrow, you have touched one of the highest concepts of prayer. If you can acknowledge that at ANY time in your experience you have KNOWN the result of prayer (that is, you have HAD a healing through spiritual means) or if, at any time in your life, you have had an evidence of the presence and power of God . . . ACTUALLY . . . you should never have to be concerned again because that ONE evidence to you of God's

presence should be ENOUGH to make you say, "Surely goodness and mercy shall follow me ALL the days of my life," ALL
the days!

How can God be with you today and not tomorrow? How
can God manifest or express Itself one day and not the next
day?

The Hebrews had a hard time learning that lesson. When
they INSISTED on picking manna for tomorrow and the day
after and the day after that, Moses had to remind them that
if that manna was falling out of the sky by the Grace of God,
WHY should they think that it wouldn't fall tomorrow and
the day after? Why should God stop as long as there was a need?

Is there a possibility that God will stop your blessings
as long as you have a need? Is it possible that the hand of God
is shortened or will be withdrawn from you before the fulfillment of your destiny? Why should you ever have to question?
Why should you ever have to treat?

Meditate on the spirit of the 23rd Psalm . . . a Psalm that
in no wise, no place, reaches out to God . . . seeks anything
from God . . . but, rather, rests so completely, so perfectly in
the confidence, the assurance, "SURELY goodness and mercy
shall follow me ALL the days of my life."

Then comes the conclusion, "And I will DWELL in the
house of the Lord forever." "I will dwell" in God consciousness "forever."

There is no treatment about it . . . just a statement, "And
I will dwell" in God consciousness . . . "in the house of the
Lord, forever."

That may be a cue for you. Have YOU made the declara-
tion, "I WILL dwell IN the house of the Lord [in God con-
sciousness] forever"?

## IF YOU WOULD PRAY

IN THE PASSAGES in *The Infinite Way* (pp. 94–98) reference is made to waking in the morning and then going all through the day in the CONSTANT recognition of the presence and power of God in every experience.

Remember the passages of scripture, "Thou wilt keep him in perfect peace whose mind is STAYED on Thee"; "Acknowledge Him in ALL thy ways and He will give thee rest"; "Quietness and confidence shall be my strength"; "I will DWELL in the house of the Lord forever."

Remember the 91st Psalm, the first verse, "He that DWELLETH in the secret place of the most high." This Psalm goes on to relate the terrible things that would NOT come nigh your dwelling place IF your dwelling place were the secret place of the most high.

Here, again, is the same idea, "I will dwell in the house of the Lord forever."

If YOU are living in the consciousness of God CONSTANTLY, you, too, can say, "The LORD is my Shepherd, I shall not want. He makes me lie down in green pastures. HE leads me beside the still waters. . . ."

If you are NOT living IN the consciousness of the presence of God, certainly you cannot expect to demonstrate the rest of the 91st Psalm or the 23rd Psalm. There again the highest concept or idea of prayer IS the recognition of God as omnipresence and omnipotence . . . the recognition of God as ever present, ever available . . . the recognition of God as the Law and the Light unto our being, BUT with no attempt to MAKE it so.

THIS is the highest concept of prayer . . . this constant DWELLING in the REALIZATION of God-presence.

No longer need you wonder, "What prayer shall I pray today?" You have prayed all the prayer there is when you pray, "I dwell in the house of the Lord now and forever."

Another verification of this is to be found in the 27th Psalm, "The Lord is my light and my salvation; WHOM shall I fear? The Lord is the strength of my life; of whom shall I be afraid? Though an host should encamp against me, my heart shall not fear. Though war should rise against me, in this will I be comforted. . . . ONE thing have I desired of the Lord . . . THAT will I seek after . . . THAT I MAY *DWELL* IN THE HOUSE OF THE LORD *ALL* THE DAYS OF MY LIFE."

There it is again. DWELLING, LIVING, MOVING and HAVING YOUR BEING in GOD CONSCIOUSNESS is PRAYER. It is the highest form of prayer there is because once you come to that constant, conscious realization of God, then you come back to your 23rd Psalm and you find you no longer have to reach out to God or pray to God . . . you merely say, "Why should I? The Lord IS my shepherd, I shall not want, He MAKETH me to lie down, of course, He MAKETH me as I have made GOD my dwelling place."

This prayer . . . this realization of prayer . . . is the one that meets ALL of our so-called needs. This is the nature of prayer that reveals our ultimate harmony to us. There is no God sitting around waiting for us to pray in any right manner or wrong manner. There is no God going to suddenly give us something He has been withholding from us.

The Lord being our shepherd, it is IMPOSSIBLE for us to want and it is impossible for God to withhold our good, our safety, our security, our protection; BUT there is a price, and it can be found in the teachings of the Master as well as in the Old Testament.

THAT PRICE IS "Dwelling in the Secret Place of the Most High" . . . LIVING in the consciousness of God, forever. That is the answer.

Another confirmation of this can be found in 2 Chronicles 32: "Be strong and courageous. Be not afraid nor dismayed for the King of Assyria . . . nor for all the multitude that is with him . . . for there be more with us than with him."

There is NO PRAYER, no reaching out to God, no trying to get God to do something. There is merely a STATEMENT.

"With him is an arm of flesh but with us is the Lord our God to help us and to fight our battles."

Then follow the most wonderful words in all scripture, "And the people rested themselves upon the WORDS of Hezekiah."

They didn't rest themselves upon their arms or ammunition, they rested themselves upon the WORDS of Hezekiah, and what were those words? "Be not afraid," the arm of flesh cannot do a thing to you because we have a God.

It is only as we LIVE constantly in that assurance of God's presence that we can say, in the face of any form of trouble, "I will not fear evil, even though I walk through the valley of the shadow of death, because I know Thou art with me. What difference does it make what experience I go through if I am SURE that God is WITH me!"

The one thing to be ever on guard against is the suggestion, through fear, that possibly God is NOT with us.

There is a story about a man who was training his small son. He took him outside, placed him on the first step and said, "Jump into Daddy's arms." The boy jumped and his Daddy caught him.

Then the father placed the boy on the second step and said, "Jump into Daddy's arms." The boy jumped again and his Daddy caught him.

Then the father placed the boy on the third step and said, "Jump into Daddy's arms." The boy jumped, but this time the father let the boy fall. The father explained, "You see, boy, never trust anybody . . . not even your Daddy."

Needless to say, after that, the boy could never feel completely assured of his father's help, nor could he know what fatherhood really means.

That is what has happened to us. Somewhere in our lives, through some experience of our own or others, we have come to the conclusion that you cannot depend on Father. When you get to that third step, there is no use trusting Him because He may not be there.

Therefore, it is necessary to go back within the innermost recesses of your own being until you reach that point of conviction that the Father IS present . . . that you do not have to fear the multitudes . . . that you do not even have to FEAR while you are in the valley of the shadow of death . . . that you need have no FEAR of lack and limitation even in the presence of your enemies.

"Thou preparest a table before me in the presence of mine enemies. Yea, though I walk through the valley of the shadow of death" I cannot be made to fear even then, since "Thou art with me."

If you would attain the highest concept of prayer, you must stop praying in the ordinary sense of WORDS. Make your prayer a CONTINUOUS REALIZATION of the presence and power of God in ALL your ways. Twenty-four hours a day KNOW that God is guiding and directing your EVERY thought, word and deed. LIVE in a constant remembrance of your beloved Father.

## ENTER THE SILENCE

SILENCE IS POWER. Silence is the healing activity in individual consciousness. Silence is the creative Principle of all existence.

In this Silence, you become receptive to the Inner Voice, the Voice of the Inner Self, and as Truth expresses Itself in your listening ear, you become aware of the Healing Influence, with signs following.

Your receptivity to the Kingdom of God, God Consciousness, God Awareness, God Knowing, constitutes a healing atmosphere.

Heretofore, the work of the student has been to bring about harmony in his experience through the statement or affirmation of Truth, or reading or quoting Truth. Now he rises higher in consciousness to where he constantly and consciously "listens" for Truth to utter Itself within him. He learns the true nature of Silence, of stillness and quietness.

It is easy to understand why the sages of old taught, "Be still, and know that I am God"; that this stillness declares the Presence of God, "Closer than breathing, nearer than hands and feet." It reveals that neither man nor circumstance nor condition can be power over your affairs, since that which declared Itself to be "I" within you is God, is Power, is Presence.

Also, you now know why you can never be God but that God is inseparable from your very being. All this reveals itself to you in The Silence.

Always remember that it is not the thoughts you think nor the truths you read, but rather, That which has revealed Itself in "quietness and confidence" is God, the Restorer of Harmony in your existence. It is not the thoughts you think but the thoughts which unfold to you within your own being

. . . these constitute your guidance and inner wisdom. It is not so much the thoughts of Truth you declare, as the consciousness of Truth you develop through your inner receptivity, that brings God-government into your body and outer affairs.

The activity of Truth in your consciousness is the Light which dispels the darkness of human sense. It is not what you think about Truth but what Truth knows and declares to you . . . not what you affirm to Divine Mind but what It reveals to you. This is The Silence. This is Power.

In quietness and confidence, in stillness and Silence, Love reveals Its comforting Presence and assures us that "underneath are the everlasting arms" upholding and supporting us, even in trial and tribulation.

The heading over the 23rd Psalm is "David's confidence in God's grace." Can you not *feel* this calm confidence as you read, "The Lord is my Shepherd; I shall not want." Here there is no petition, no supplication and, above all, no doubt or fear. Since the Lord IS his Shepherd, HOW can he want?

"He maketh me to lie down in green pastures; He leadeth me beside the still waters." (The peace that passeth understanding enfolds me as I realize I cannot escape from my good, since He not only provides me with green pastures but He MAKETH me to lie down in them; He not only gives me still waters but He LEADETH me beside the still calm waters of peace.)

"He restoreth my soul." (Even though it has been scarlet with sin or unrestful in sickness, yet "He restoreth my soul; He leadeth me in the paths of righteousness for His name's sake," and though I still be tempted with desire, yet for His name's sake He leadeth me out of sin into righteousness, out of disease into rightness of health.)

"Yea, though I walk through the valley of the shadow of death, I will fear no evil, for Thou art with me; Thy rod and Thy staff they comfort me." (David's confidence in God's grace is still felt, even in the valley of the shadow of death, since even here David feels no fear, "for Thou art with me." Oh, God, that I too may "be still" and know no fear, since even in the valley of the shadow of death "Thou art with me.")

You can only experience fear if you believe that, in the midst of your discords and inharmonies, God has deserted you. NEVER, in scarlet sin nor dangerous disease, will you fear, once you attain David's confidence that even in the valley of the shadow of death "Thou art with me." Let the Beloved Silence descend upon you, too, as you realize with all your being that "Thou art with me."

"Thy rod and Thy staff they comfort me." (God's grace, always manifest in the human form of rod, staff, food or water, this grace appearing as my good, comforts me. This assurance of the presence of that which fulfills, protects, sustains . . . this comforts me.)

"Thou preparest a table before me in the presence of mine enemies; Thou anointest my head with oil; my cup runneth over." (Where lack and limitation threaten, God's grace prevails; my soul is filled with inspiration and my heart overflows with joy and gratitude. This evidence of abundance, through Grace, fills me . . . satisfies me . . . and my heart sings for joy in His Presence.)

"Surely goodness and mercy shall follow me all the days of my life and I will dwell in the House of the Lord forever." (How confident, how positive is David, as he sings, "Surely goodness and mercy shall follow me," and how secure he feels in the timelessness of God's Grace, as he declares that this goodness and mercy "shall follow me all the days of my life."

Blessed assurance of Omnipresence, "ALL the days of my life." And, of course, "I will dwell in this consciousness of God forever. Yes, God Consciousness shall be my home forever.")

"The former things have passed away" and "All things are become new." "Whereas I was blind, now I see" and not "through a glass, darkly" but "face to face." Yes, even in my flesh I have seen God. The hills have rolled away and there is no more horizon but the light of heaven makes all things plain.

Long have I sought Thee, O Jerusalem, but only now have my pilgrim feet touched the soil of heaven. The waste places are no more. Fertile lands are before me, the like of which I have never dreamed. Oh, truly, "There shall be no night there." The glory of it shines as the noonday sun. There is no need of light, for God is the light thereof.

I sit down to rest. In the shade of trees I rest and find my peace in Thee. Within Thy Grace is peace, O Lord. In the world I was weary, in Thee I have found rest. In the dense forest of words I was lost, in the letter of Truth was tiredness and fear . . . but in Thy Spirit ONLY is shade and water and rest.

How far have I wandered from Thy Spirit, O Tender One and True, how far, how far. How deeply lost I have been in the maze of words . . . words . . . words. But now am I returned, and in Thy Spirit shall I ever find my life, my peace, my strength. Thy Spirit is the Bread of Life, finding which, I shall never hunger again. Thy Spirit is a well-spring of water, drinking which, I shall never thirst again.

As a weary wanderer I have sought Thee and now my weariness is gone. Thy Spirit has formed a tent for me, and in its cool shade I linger. Peace fills my soul. Thy Presence has filled me with peace. Thy love has placed before me a Feast of Spirit.

Yes, Thy Spirit is my resting place, an oasis in the desert of the letter of Truth.

In Thee will I hide from the noise of the world of argument, in Thy Consciousness find surcease from the noisomeness of men's tongues. They divide Thy Garment, O Lord of Peace, they quarrel over Thy Word until It becomes words and no longer Word.

As a beggar have I sought the new heaven and the new earth, and Thou hast made me heir of all. How shall I stand before Thee but in Silence? How shall I honor Thee but in the MEDITATION of my heart?

Praise and thanksgiving Thou seekest not, but the understanding heart Thou receivest. I will keep silent before Thee. My Soul and my Spirit and my Silence shall be Thy Dwelling Place. Thy Spirit shall fill my meditation, and It shall make me and preserve me whole. O Tender One and True, I am Home in Thee.

# Love

## THE EXERCISE OF LOVE

LET BROTHERLY LOVE continue.

Be not forgetful to entertain strangers: for thereby some have entertained angels unawares.

Remember them that are in bonds, as bound with them; and them which suffer adversity, as being yourselves also in the body. . . .

Let your conversation be without covetousness; and be content with such things as ye have: for he hath said, I will never leave thee, nor forsake thee.

So that we may boldly say, The Lord is my helper, and I will not fear what man shall do unto me.

Remember them which have the rule over you, who have spoken unto you the word of God: whose faith follow, considering the end of their conversation.

Jesus Christ the same yesterday, and today, and forever.

Be not carried about with divers and strange doctrines. For it is a good thing that the heart be established with grace. . . .

Hebrews, ch. 13


Let every soul be subject unto the higher powers. For there is no power but of God: the powers that be are ordained of God.

Whosoever therefore resisteth the power, resisteth the ordinance of God. . . .

For rulers are not a terror to good works, but to the evil. Wilt thou then not be afraid of the power? do that which is good, and thou shalt have praise of the same:

For he is the minister of God to thee for good.

Romans, ch. 13


Love not only IS God but Love is OF God and it manifests itself to us through man.

It might better be said that Love, which is God, manifests itself AS man, for Love is the offspring of God even as man is.

Love, in human experience, seems to be a difficult experience. Looking out upon the world, it would appear that Love is not as prevalent as it might be, that Love is not given and received as it might be. Perhaps we, ourselves, have been partly responsible for this.

Through the ages, we have been taught to be more loving, to be more kind, to be more just. Strangely enough, it does not lie within our power to do that.

At any given moment of our experience, we are as loving and as kind, as merciful and charitable as it is possible to be from that point of consciousness at that moment. For someone to say, "Be MORE loving, be MORE kind, be MORE just," is asking that of us which is impossible.

We and the whole world are giving out love to the full extent of our present capacity.

There IS a way in which we can be more loving, more kind, more just, more charitable, and there IS a way to bring forth more Love from the world, but that way is not by looking to each other FOR it. THAT way lies disappointment.

To ask of each other that we be more loving is NOT the way. Every man and every woman on the face of the earth is being as loving as he knows how to be.

There is only one way to increase that love and that is the way which, if we understood it, would bring peace on earth and good will to all men, and nothing else will. Every HUMAN attempt to bring peace on earth has failed, and failed over a period of thousands of years.

There remains but one way to bring peace on earth and that is through spiritual means. Instead of looking to each other for Love, let us forget each other and let us look to God for Love.

Let us lift our gaze over the heads of our fellow men and REALIZE that since God is Love, ALL Love MUST flow forth FROM God . . . NOT FROM MAN . . . FROM GOD.

It is true that Love flows THROUGH man, but we only open the avenues of Love through each other by not looking to each other for it but by looking to God for it. The moment we expect Love from each other, we may get hate or indifference. We may find Love today and indifference tomorrow.

The moment we look to each other for justice we may find a measure of it, but we may also find injustice, inequality. There is no way known to bring out justice from a man by expecting it from him. Those who have had experience with law courts can well testify that it isn't even easy to find it on the Bench.

The reason for this is that selfish motives impel most of us just as in our voting at the polls most of us vote according to the way in which we think we will derive the greatest benefit. Rarely do we set aside our personal interests and consider that which would be for the best interests of the Nation. We seldom rise to such heights of unselfishness.

So it is whenever we look for justice, mercy, kindness. We are most apt to find self-interest . . . UNTIL we rise above that place where we seek our good from man.

## THE SOURCE OF LOVE

ONCE YOU EXPERIENCE the satisfaction of saying, "I shall not fear what man can do to me, nor will I look to man for praise, for honor, for glory, but to God. I will not look to man for kindness, courtesy, consideration, but to God," you will then find that you have touched the SOURCE of Love, the source of Life, the source of Good.

As you continue to focus your attention solely on God, Love begins to flow TO you THROUGH man . . . AS man. Not always does Love come through those to whom we are looking for it. Not always does Love come through those from whom we may expect it. However, this becomes of very little importance as we grow in our understanding of Love.

In this life, what everyone wants is Love. We want the opportunity of receiving it. We want the opportunity of expressing it.

At first, we may feel some disappointment at not finding it in those, from those, from whom we have the right to expect it. However, that soon passes and we learn to be grateful for the fact that now our lives are filled with Love, Joy, Peace,

Consideration, Cooperation, and we learn to accept it from those whom God gives to us.

It would be possible in just a very few months, at most a very few years, to bring Peace on Earth, if everywhere we were taught not to expect it of man, of nations, of politicians, of government heads, of peace bodies, but to look for it in the ONLY place it can be found . . . IN GOD.

*Let EVERY soul be subject unto the HIGHER powers.*
*For there is NO power but of God.*

Romans 13:1

Let us be subject unto God for our Love, just as in the Infinite Way teaching we subject ourselves to God for our Life. We declare, "God is Life Eternal. God is Infinite. Therefore Life Eternal is Infinite and THAT Life IS my life."

In that same way, we must be subject unto God for Love. We must NOT be subject unto man or unto woman or child. We must be subject unto God ONLY for Love.

Love is of God. Let us therefore look to God for Love and welcome it as it comes to us THROUGH our fellow man. It is in this way that we sometimes entertain angels unawares.

If we are not looking to this individual or to that individual but to God, we will find that the stranger in our midst IS the emissary of God, BRINGING Love to us.

## LOVE KNOWS NO LIMITATION

WE CLOSE THE DOOR on Love when we expect it ONLY from our husband or wife or child or parents or neighbor or friend.

We close the door on Love in that way when we pray ONLY for Mother or Father or child or friend or relative.

When we learn to pray for our enemy as we are taught to do in the Master's teachings, when we learn to pray the prayer of forgiveness for all those who offend us, we then find Love coming to us through unexpected avenues and channels.

We, ourselves, limit the amount of Love that ordinarily would be flowing freely to us because we limit it, first of all, to man, and secondly, only to those men and women who comprise our friendly circle.

When we go further afield, when we look not only to friends but even to foes for our Love, through the prayer of forgiveness, we widen that circle, and even more so as we realize God is the fount of ALL Love . . . God is the SOURCE of ALL Love.

Therefore, it is to God and ONLY to God that we look for Love. This applies not only to Love as the great word but also to the infinite ramifications of Love.

## LOVE IS SUPPLY

SUPPLY IS AN ACTIVITY of Love. We have limited our supply if we have limited it to our positions, our marriages, our inheritances, instead of realizing that supply is actually an activity of Love.

ALL of the supply that ever took place in Scripture came about through the Love of God for His Creation and through the Love of the prophets, saints and seers of God. THAT Love became manifest as substance.

Therefore, supply IS an activity of Love, and if we limit that to the human avenues of expression, we limit the amount of supply that can come to us. Once we lift our gaze above the human avenues and channels of supply and realize GOD as the source of Love and, therefore, as the source of supply, we begin to open the way for Love to come to us from many new sources.

## FORGIVENESS

WE HAVE LOOKED to man for forgiveness for our offenses, our trespasses, our sins. Often, through acts of commission or omission, we have been unloving, unjust, unkind; and sometimes, if possible, we look to those whom we have offended for forgiveness.

In many instances, they have gone so far out of our experience that we have no way of reaching them in order to seek their forgiveness.

Actually, there is no need of our seeking forgiveness of any man. It is well that we apologize, if we have offended. It is well if we ask forgiveness. It is not important whether or not we receive it.

The important point is that we look to GOD for forgiveness . . . NOT to man. As long as we look to God for forgiveness, we will be released through man.

Therein lies the miracle . . . that even those who, to human sense, would withhold forgiveness, can no longer withhold it when we have sought it in God.

## LOVE IS PRACTICAL

IT IS A STRANGE THING but ALL of human experience is a looking to each other for something. ALL of SPIRITUAL experience is a looking to GOD for EVERYTHING.

At first, this is a deep, transitional phase of experience. As we begin the study and practice of The Infinite Way, it is difficult.

It is difficult for the salesman going out to sell to raise himself above the belief that the prospect or the customer has the power to GIVE the order or to WITHHOLD it. From the human standpoint, it would seem that the buyer has the power to give or withhold, but it is not true. We limit the amount of orders we receive by just such a belief. We increase them infinitely when we realize that NO MAN has the power to give or to withhold. ALL POWER IS IN GOD!

When we understand this, we can say, "Thank you, Father. Thank you, even that they did not buy." We can say this because it was the Divine Hand that withheld them and kept them from making what might have been a mistake for them.

However, this would in no wise LIMIT our sales.

The same law applies when we go to court. We limit ourselves when we look to judge or to jury for mercy or for justice. These things are not to be found there. There is only a limited human sense of mercy and justice in even the best judge or jury.

However, if we enter the court in the realization that GOD is Love, GOD is Mercy, GOD is Justice, GOD is the seat and source of ALL authority; as we keep our gaze on that One Infinite Being, the source of our Life, the source of our Love, the source of our justice and benevolence, we find it REFLECTED in judge and jury . . . sometimes even to their own astonishment.

So it is in every walk of life we have been accustomed to looking to MAN for intelligence. We have even become accustomed to expecting the automobile driver on the road to be a good driver. This is not possible. We can only be good drivers now and then.

However, this is not so in our experience when we realize GOD as the Intelligence of the road; GOD as the Principle, the Law; GOD as the ONLY Driver on the road. In this realization we will experience, not only in our own driving, but in the driving of all those we encounter on the road, Intelligence and Love.

Understand this . . . you must not expect good driving from the drivers on the road. You will only find a proportion of it. However, you will find every single driver to be intelligent and loving when you do not expect that of him . . . when you expect that ONLY OF GOD.

When you understand GOD as the One Ruling Mind and Intelligence of the Universe, looking to That Mind for Wisdom, Guidance, Direction and Protection, you receive it at the hands of EVERY individual.

LOOKING TO GOD for Life, instead of to bread and to meat, we find Life. We find Life Eternal.

LOOKING TO GOD for Love, instead of to man, we find that Love REFLECTED to us through those we meet.

LOOKING TO GOD for Infinite Wisdom and Intelligence, we find it on the road, in business, in court, WHEREVER WE MAY BE.

It is not difficult to bring about this change if we remember this:

All HUMAN experience is looking to each other.

All SPIRITUAL experience is looking to God.

Remember this as a constant reminder, should you be looking to man, whose breath is in his nostrils; should you be looking to princes, to favoritism, to politics, to man. Look ONLY to God and you will find there the REAL meaning of Love.

Man cannot GIVE Love and man cannot WITHHOLD Love, but the kind of Love that we receive THROUGH man when we look to God for it is the kind of Love that makes us eternally happy, joyous, and it is an unchanging Love. It isn't Love today and indifference or hate tomorrow. It is Love at every level of human experience but an ever expanding Love.

## SEEK SPIRITUAL DISCRIMINATION

As LOVE MANIFESTS ITSELF in our experience, we have a measuring rod for discerning whether it is HUMAN Love or DIVINE Love that we are expressing.

As we live in our homes, in our businesses, in our community and are called upon for expressions of Love in one way or another, we can always ask ourselves, "Do I expect a return?" If we do, it is human Love, finite Love, and a very unsatisfactory Love.

No one ever derives a great joy, even from a gift, even from an expression of Love, when he knows that someone is waiting there for a return.

The Love that gives true satisfaction and joy is the Love we know we didn't deserve and for which no return is expected. It comes straight from the heart with no desire for a return.

That is the guide for us.

As we express our sense of duty to our family, to our friends, to our community, to each other, we must be sure that we are not seeking thanks, appreciation, reward, recognition or praise. Be not afraid, you will have all of these.

The error lies in SEEKING it or EXPECTING it. It is not really Love at all when we express or give it for the purpose or in the expectancy of a return. It is a trade . . . like the modern Christmas. It is more of a trade than an expression of Love.

It is possible to perform every family duty without really feeling, "Ah, yes, but in return I am entitled to this." It is not easy because we have been brought up the other way.

However, in turning from the HUMAN sense of experience to the SPIRITUAL (that IS what we are trying to do in our Infinite Way Life—we are trying to emulate the example of The Master; that is the ONLY reason why we are in this work) we start with that idea of letting this Love flow while performing our duties, without looking to the individual for a return, letting the Love express itself as it will.

As we do that and expect our return (whatever return may be necessary) from God, expect our Love from God, we find new relationships on earth.

From the moment you can accept the idea in your mind that LOVE IS OF GOD and the only place to look for it is in and from God and, therefore, whatever of Love you express is God expressing Itself and so you need not take credit for it nor expect a return from it, from that time you enter an entirely new consciousness of life . . . one that has different values and one that will explain to you the meaning of Heaven on Earth, because Earth does become transposed into some degree, at least, of Heaven.

Insofar as we can, let us train ourselves and discipline ourselves to LET GOD express Its Love THROUGH us with no idea of return. Look NOT to man, whose breath is in his nostrils, for Love. Rather, expect it as the omnipresent activity of Divine Love.

# Gratitude

## THE MEANING OF GRATITUDE

IT HAS BEEN SAID that "By their works ye shall know them." This truth applies most aptly to Gratitude. Gratitude reflects itself in works. The higher the concept of Gratitude . . . the greater the works of the Being reflecting that Gratitude.

The act of expressing Gratitude is in truth the act of recognizing and acknowledging (within yourself) the Source of all your good . . . which is God. It is impossible to express Gratitude without expressing Love, as they are both components of God and, therefore, inseparable from God.

Gratitude is akin to Love.

Gratitude, like Love, is God expressing Itself through man as man.

It is impossible to love without expressing some degree of God through your consciousness, and so it is, also, with Gratitude. It is impossible to BE grateful without expressing some degree of God while you are BEING grateful, for Gratitude is of God . . . not of man.

Gratitude has a meaning far beyond the word gratitude, itself, or even any idea connected with gratitude. It goes deep into the reality of being.

Gratitude, as it is generally understood, of course, is an outpouring in appreciation for that which we have received. Gratitude SEEMS to express our appreciation for benefits received but, actually, such is not the Truth about Gratitude.

The Truth about Gratitude is this . . . you cannot be grateful and you cannot be ungrateful. It does not lie within the power of any individual to be grateful or to express gratitude . . . nor does it lie within the power of anyone to withhold gratitude.

GRATITUDE HAS NOTHING TO DO WITH MAN.

Gratitude is one of the many phases or aspects of Love . . . and Love is God . . . therefore, Gratitude is really a form of God activity or God expression. It is, therefore, true that ONLY God can express Love . . . ONLY God can express Gratitude. We can only be the vehicles through which God pours Itself as Love or as Gratitude.

## GRATITUDE AS RELATED TO SUPPLY

GRATITUDE IS CLOSELY AKIN to the subject of supply.

How many times have you heard people say, "Oh! I wish this could be ten times more" or "If I really were expressing my gratitude as I feel it . . . this would be a million dollars."

The point here is that gratitude and supply are kindred subjects. If a person had all the supply he wanted, he might believe he would express his gratitude in greater measure. This is not true at all.

Anyone could express his gratitude to the FULLEST, if he understood gratitude in its true sense and he could express his gratitude with SUPPLY to the fullest extent, if he understood the subject of supply.

There is no limit to the Gratitude we can express since Gratitude is of God.

There is no limit to the Love we can express since Love is of God.

There is no limit to the Supply we can express, even in the form of dollars, since Supply is of God.

The main point that we forget is that GOD is individual Being . . . GOD is individual You . . . and, therefore, you have God-capacity and nothing LESS than God-capacity. You have no capacity of your own. Jesus said,

> *Why callest thou me good?*
> *There is none good but one,*
> *That is, God.*
> Matthew 19:17

We, as individuals, have no personal capacities . . . we have no personal limitations . . . and we have no personal large amounts in any way, shape, manner or form.

God is Infinite but God is individual Being . . . God is your Being . . . and that is the point that we miss in our treatments . . . in our healing work . . . and in our daily living. We continuously set up a selfhood apart from God. Even while in our treatment, we declare, "I and the Father are One. All that the Father hath is mine. I wish this check were bigger." It is not consistent.

If we really want to be consistent in our spiritual approach to life and understand that GOD IS MY INDIVIDUAL BEING and we want to express gratitude (assuming that we only have a dollar bill with which to do it at the moment), we do not apologize for that dollar bill nor do we minimize the dollar bill but we let that dollar bill go forth with all the love that we can feel . . . all the joy that we can feel . . . sending it forth with no apologies . . . no explanations. Here is, at the present moment, your sense of your God-capacity . . . that is ALL. It has no limitation and there is no desire to have it increased because it is the Allness of God coming through at this moment and when you realize that . . . that makes room for the Infinite to manifest Itself on greater and greater planes . . . greater and greater amounts . . . as the unfoldment continues.

Never judge from appearances or you will be limiting your capacity. If you look at your pocketbook, you are judging from appearances. If you even judge of your physical strength, you are judging from appearances . . . and you are limiting yourself . . . both to the amount of your bank account and to the amount of your physical strength.

By looking beyond the appearance, you realize that God is individual Being . . . God is individual You . . . the Mind of God is your Mind and, therefore, you are limited in intelligence only to the Wisdom of the Divine Mind . . . NOTHING LESS. It is true that much Wisdom may not seem to be pouring out of you at this particular moment but that has nothing to do with it. You still must not limit your capacity. Your capacity is God-capacity since God is your Mind.

You MUST live ETERNALLY . . . since GOD is your LIFE. Judge not by appearances. It is possible you might look into a mirror and find that you look ten or twenty years older than your age. You must not judge by that appearance. You must continue to HOLD to the TRUTH . . . that you have only the age of God since God is your Life . . . God is ETERNALLY your Life . . . since, before Abraham was, God is your Life and God will be your Life unto the end of the world. Therefore, your Life can know no age . . . no limitation.

Since GOD is the Substance of your Being . . . your supply must be Infinite. There is no need to look in your pocketbook or your bank account to see how closely you are approximating that in demonstration. Judge NOT by appearances . . . STAND ON THE TRUTH THAT . . . since God is the Substance of your Being, God is Infinite, your Substance is likewise Infinite.

Then, if you spend one dollar, you will think of it as THAT Infinity pouring forth as THAT dollar . . . but STILL the Infinity. That makes room for it to become two or twenty or two hundred dollars . . . but not by limiting . . . not by judging . . . but by understanding that GOD IS my Substance . . . God is Infinite, therefore, my Substance and my Supply are Infinite. Thus, in paying out even one dollar you are giving out Infinity.

## GRATITUDE AS RELATED TO LOVE

LOVE HAS TO DO with Gratitude. Love has to do with Supply. Love has to do with caring and protecting. Statements of Truth with reference to Love may also be applied to Gratitude as both are attributes of God, the same as Life, Peace, Joy, Harmony, etc.

How much Love can we express? How foolish it is to say, "I wish I could be more loving" or "I would like to be more loving." It is ridiculous. You cannot be MORE loving . . . you cannot be LESS loving . . . since God is the ONLY loving you possess.

God is Infinite . . . therefore, you possess INFINITE Love, and INFINITE Love is expressed FROM you and TO you.

This is the point that wrecks most of our lives: We believe that there are those who could GIVE us more love and we believe that there are those who are WITHHOLDING love from us. This is a fatal error.

No one can give us any more love than they are giving, and no one has the power to withhold love.

LOVE is GOD EXPRESSING Itself!

God cannot express Itself finitely. God cannot express Itself in a limited form or a limited way or in a limited amount. The error has been that you are looking to a person for Love, and a person does not HAVE Love to GIVE. Love is of God. In fact, Love IS God. In fact, God IS Love.

If you look to a person for love, you will find often, in place of love . . . hate . . . or you will find a love that TURNS to hate. The error, then, is NOT the other person's . . . the error is NOT on the part of those who WITHHOLD love . . . or SEEM to withhold. The error is on OUR part in EXPECTING love from a person . . . or in CONDEMNING him for WITH-HOLDING love. He cannot withhold what is not his . . . he cannot give what is not his.

Love is of God. The moment we turn our thought FROM the idea that a PERSON can give or withhold love . . . we FIND love pouring itself out to us in Infinite abundance . . . although not always from those from whom we have been expecting it . . . or not always from those from whom we have the right to expect it.

It does not lie within our ability to change people in their demonstration. ALL we can change is OUR demonstration.

If we are not receiving enough love in the world, let us stop looking to people for it and look to God for it. It will appear, though not always through the person from whom you expect it. That is one of the things that we must learn . . . that it is not up to us to DETERMINE from what direction Love is to come . . . it MUST come from God.

## LOOK NOT TO MAN

IT IS NOT UP TO US to DETERMINE from what direction Gratitude is to come . . . it MUST come from God.

The individual who has learned the Wisdom of GOD as Love, looks to God to express Itself even in what we call gratitude . . . sharing. As we keep our vision on God as the source of our supply . . . on God even as the source of the gratitude that must come to us . . . Gratitude COMES . . . not always from those who SHOULD be giving the most of it . . . but it COMES.

Who are we to judge who the channel should be . . . or the vehicle . . . or the avenue . . . today or tomorrow? Sufficient for us IF we are EXPERIENCING the Love of God made manifest as Gratitude . . . the Love of God made manifest as sharing . . . cooperation . . . joy . . . the Love of God made manifest as Love . . . without our trying to DETERMINE . . . who? . . . when? . . . or how much?

Healing work will be very simple ONCE you begin to realize that God is individual Being and NO person has the capacity to BE sick. No person has the capacity to be sick . . . or to be well. God is the ONE Divine Life . . . the ONLY Life . . . and It is individual Life . . . YOUR Life . . . and because It is God . . . It has no capacity to be sick. It has no capacity to be weak.

Therefore, as you learn to keep your vision on GOD as individual Being . . . as YOUR Being . . . you will find NOTHING in your Being ". . . that defileth . . . or maketh a lie." (Revelation 21:27)

AGAIN, we must not judge by appearances. At this present moment, ALL of us (in appearance) are showing forth some phase of discord . . . inharmony . . . ill health . . . lack. The

REASON is that we have not FULLY realized God as individual Being. We STILL have a selfhood apart from God.

As long as we look to someone outside of ourselves for love . . . gratitude . . . supply . . . we have not REALIZED that God is our own individual Being. Therefore, we have no right to look OUT THERE for love . . . gratitude . . . or supply. We must ONLY look to God . . . THE God of our own Being . . . NOT OUT THERE . . . NOT in our homes . . . only to the God of our own Being. THEN . . . let it come through whom it will . . . or from whatever direction it will.

If we look to the God of another Being . . . we look amiss. We should look to the God of our OWN Being. GOD is individual Being . . . GOD is YOUR individual Being. Therefore, God is pouring Its Love TO you . . . THROUGH you . . . AS you . . . OUT into the world. This is true of EVERY individual.

As long as you have God (and the Kingdom of God is WITHIN YOU) . . . as long as you have the ENTIRE Kingdom of God within YOU, pouring Itself forth as Love . . . Joy . . . Companionship . . . Supply . . . Gratitude . . . WHY should you be looking out there for it? As long as you do not look out there for it, SOMEBODY out there . . . or MANY bodies . . . WILL be the vehicles or avenues bringing it to your door. LOOKING OUT THERE for it is the error.

GOD is individual Being. GOD is YOUR individual Being. It is RIGHT to ask the practitioner or the teacher for help . . . but it is also right to understand that THAT help is coming from the God of your OWN Being . . . from the Kingdom of God within YOU.

Every experience to you in your life is YOUR OWN CONSCIOUSNESS of Truth unfolding . . . whether it comes to you as Love . . . whether it comes to you as Supply . . . or Gratitude . . . or Success . . . or Health. Regardless of whom it

SEEMS to come through . . . it may be husband or wife, parent or child, or a friend . . . it is YOUR OWN CONSCIOUSNESS of TRUTH unfolding.

The moment YOU realize God as individual Being . . . the moment you realize God as YOUR individual Being . . . the Infinity of Good MUST unfold from WITHIN YOU . . . THROUGH YOU . . . TO the world . . . nothing LESS than Infinity. Then you never have to apologize, because you never lack . . . you never have an insufficiency . . . whether it is of strength . . . whether it is of healing power . . . whether it is of understanding . . . whether it is of gratitude . . . or whether it is of supply.

You cannot have an insufficiency of any kind IF your Source is God . . . THAT makes the Source of it Infinite. When you personalize it and set up a selfhood apart from God . . . then . . . when you are called on to feed four thousand, five thousand and women and children, too . . . you cannot do it. You explain that you do not have that many farms or storehouses or barns . . . you do not have that many bonds or bank accounts. You have set up this personal selfhood and expect it to meet the demands that are made upon you. Naturally, you fail to meet the need.

You might just as well be a practitioner and have a hundred people come to you with various diseases and you respond by saying, "Oh . . . Oh . . . I couldn't possibly heal all these people of all these diseases." Certainly, you could not . . . of yourself. You have nothing to do it with . . . BUT . . . in the understanding of God as the REAL Law of Being, you have the Capacity of God to do the healing and you can heal multitudes.

No one knows what demands may be made upon them tomorrow or in the near future. You may be called upon to feed many hundreds of people or you may be called upon to heal many thousands of people and you wonder where the supply or the healing is going to come from. It is going to come from God . . . THROUGH YOU . . . once you realize that God IS your individual Being and EVERY demand made upon you can be fulfilled.

NO demand can EVER be made upon you for Love, Joy, Gratitude or Supply that you cannot fulfill, since it is not of you . . . it is of God. If necessary, there will be a multiplication of loaves and fishes but YOU won't multiply them any more than Jesus did. GOD WILL DO THE WORK.

Jesus looked up to the Father and the loaves and the fishes were multiplied. In other words, Jesus recognized, "I can of my own self do nothing but the Father WITHIN ME multiplies the loaves and fishes . . . and even produces gold in the fishes' mouths."

When you realize God to be your CAPACITY, you have INFINITE capacity. Then, despite appearances, never apologize . . . never explain . . . just hold to the Truth of Being. Never apologize for a limitation. Never apologize for a lack of demonstration.

## RECOGNITION AND ACKNOWLEDGMENT

NO ONE HAS THE RIGHT . . . at this particular stage of unfoldment . . . to expect any of us to be the FULL Christhead. Anyone of us may achieve it today or tomorrow . . . and there may be some among us who HAVE achieved it . . . but they are not known to the public at large. However, we may be assured of this . . . that we HAVE achieved a wonderful measure of it in Truth work and in our understanding . . . and

. . . regardless of what inharmony or discord presents itself today, we have a WONDERFUL thing with which to meet it.

What is that WONDERFUL THING? The REALIZATION of GOD as individual BEING.

As we continue to progress in that unfoldment and gain greater and greater realizations of it, we will show forth greater demonstrations of it . . . ONLY, however, IF we can begin with a Principle. We MUST know WHAT the Principle is . . . and the Principle begins with the word GOD . . . NOT God separate and apart from you . . . NOT you separate and apart from God . . . but GOD as YOUR individual BEING . . . the Divine Mind as your individual Mind . . . the one Infinite Life as your individual Life . . . the one Divine Substance as the Substance even of your body . . . of your being . . . of your business . . . of ALL that concerns YOU.

THAT understanding of ONENESS, accepted even intellectually, BEGINS to be the foundation of the spiritual apprehension of the idea . . . and it is the SPIRITUAL DISCERNMENT that results in demonstration.

Often we NEED this letter . . . this correct letter of Truth . . . for our foundation. We must KNOW what the Principle is that we are trying to demonstrate . . . and the Principle IS God . . . as your individual Being . . . God, as your Capacity . . . God, as the amount of ALL that concerns you . . . God, as the amount of your supply . . . God, as the amount of your gratitude . . . God, as the amount of your love.

Why should you be limited in expressing love if it is not you expressing at all but rather God expressing Itself—?

Why should love be limited in its expression to you if you are looking to God to express Itself as Love?

As long as you keep looking to God to express Itself as Love, you MUST receive the FULL MEASURE of God-Love.

When you limit it to a person's capacity to express love . . . or when you limit your supply to the amount of a person's bank account . . . you are lost. REALIZE THIS!

In ALL relationships, do not look to each other as though THAT person could give or withhold. It is of the utmost importance that we realize, at all times, that we are not looking to a person but to the Christ of his Being and of our Being.

It is for this reason that at some period in our study we must make a CONSCIOUS exercise along this line (call it a discipline, if you will): at some period we must agree that EVERYONE we meet in the course of the day is Christ. As we get up in the morning and greet members of our family, do not dwell on personalities by liking this one and disliking that one and finding fault with another one. Rather, secretly, inwardly, greet each one as The Christ.

As we leave home and go to the market or the stores or business, all whom we meet we must CONSCIOUSLY recognize as The Christ. The Christ of you greets the Christ of them. The Christ of you loves the Christ of them. The Christ of them loves the Christ of you. In our Christhood we are One. We are not looking at appearances now. We are not thinking of male or female. We are not thinking of what we must give or what we shall receive. We are thinking only of TRUE IDENTITY.

Are we expecting even COURTESY from store people? We have no right to, because they do not have it to give . . . they do not have it to withhold. Only The Christ expresses Itself AS Courtesy. Therefore, we should look to The Christ of each one, and not to the outer. Otherwise, it would be the same as if we were looking at a cluster of electric lights and expecting the light from the bulbs. The light is not there at all. The light is an emanation of the electricity.

If we were to limit ourselves by looking to the bulb for light, sooner or later we would be disappointed, as the bulb would burn out and we would be without light . . . BUT, as long as we are looking to the electricity, we will have light, even if we have to produce a new bulb.

So it is with us. If we are looking to GOD for Love, we will always have it . . . BUT . . . if we are looking to PERSONS for love, they may burn out or they may turn to hate . . . indifference . . . ingratitude.

If we are looking to GOD, whatever happens out here in this scene (the visible world) will make no difference. This one may get washed away . . . that one may turn away . . . Judas will betray . . . Peter will deny . . . Thomas will doubt . . . BUT IT WILL MAKE NO DIFFERENCE. We expected nothing of Judas . . . we expected nothing of Peter . . . we expected nothing of Thomas. ALL we expected was of GOD.

What happens to Judas? He commits suicide . . . and a twelfth one is appointed to take his place. The work goes right on. The love goes right on. The ministry goes right on because the Minister . . . God . . . is there. What happens to Judas? Who cares?

What happens to those who betray . . . slander . . . defame . . . or are ungrateful? Who cares? They are living in accord with the law:

*Be not deceived; God is not mocked: for whatsoever*
*a man soweth, that shall he also reap.*

Galatians 6:7


That is not your demonstration . . . it is their demonstration.

## AS WE SOW

WE, TOO, ARE LIVING in accord with the law of "As we sow, so shall we reap."

IF WE SOW to GOD AS the source of our good, we will reap infinite, eternal good . . . regardless of what happens to all the people in our experience.

Scripture says, "When my father and my mother forsake me, then the Lord will take me up." (Psalm 27:10)

It is possible for fathers and mothers to forsake children and it is possible for children to forsake parents, and so we have no right to look to father or mother or children. OUR looking . . . OUR sowing should ALWAYS be to God.

If you sow to the Spirit you will reap Spiritual Good, and if you sow to the flesh you will reap corruption.

If you sow, if you expect your good from man, whose breath is in his nostrils, sooner or later you must meet with Judas . . . with doubting Thomas . . . with the denying Peter. As a matter of fact, even if you do not have that experience, you will probably have all twelve disciples go to sleep on you. It is not always downright evil that betrays us. It can be just something like that . . . going to sleep on the job.

When we look to person, place or thing for gratitude . . . for supply . . . for love . . . for companionship . . . anything that happened to Jesus through his disciples can happen to us through those to whom we look. That is the lesson Jesus gave us through the disciples. Each served his purpose in proportion to his capacity but not one of them endured.

However, Jesus' principle of Life eternal endured because even without the twelve disciples, He still walked out of the tomb and walked out in His own body . . . the same body that had been wounded. His Principle did not betray Him . . . nor did His Principle forsake Him. Even if it were true that He had spoken those words, "Why hast Thou forsaken me?" we know that was merely a temporary weakness caused by His disappointment at the failure of all His disciples. He quickly realized, however, that His Principle had not forsaken Him because He walked out of the tomb.

So it is with us. God is individual Being, and since God is Love . . . Love is Infinite in Being. Therefore, you can know nothing less than an infinity of Love.

God is Mind . . . But God is Divine Mind. Therefore, you can know nothing less than an infinity of Wisdom . . . Intelligence . . . Guidance . . . Direction.

God is Substance. Therefore, you can know nothing less than Infinite Substance . . . and so on through all the synonyms.

Once you grasp the idea of God as individual Being, you will solve all the problems of so-called human existence. Then you will find that Gratitude is not something that you can give or withhold. It is something that God expresses through you. When you try to limit it or even to increase it, you are getting in the way of God's activity.


## CORRECT YOUR CONCEPTS

NOW WE COME to the ultimate of this subject which began with just Gratitude. Let us consider the point that, when Jesus walked out of the tomb, it was with the same body that had been crucified . . . in which the wounds were still apparent.

The moment you understand God as individual Being . . . God as the Substance of all form . . . you will understand that your body is Spiritual and that your body is just as Infinite and just as Eternal as your Gratitude . . . as your Supply . . . as your Love. Your body does not differ from your love. Your body does not differ from your supply or your gratitude or your benevolence or your cooperation or your sharing or your wisdom. Your body is as infinite and as eternal as God since God is the Substance thereof. God is the Substance of which your body is formed.

Therefore, for one reason or another, through ignorance or desire, should you experience what we know as death or transition or passing on (it makes no difference what name you use . . . a rose, by any other name, is just as sweet) you will find just what Jesus demonstrated . . . that you have not left a body here for burial or for cremation . . . you have taken your body with you . . . and all its wounds with it too. The form of your body will change in proportion to your ascending consciousness of Truth.

Jesus knew that His body was eternal. He knew that it was immortal. Understanding this, He knew that the crucifixion could not destroy His Life or His Body. Jesus' wisdom was greater than the understanding of those who believe that Life is Spirit . . . Life is God . . . Life is Eternal . . . but that Life inhabits a material body.

Jesus knew that there was only one Creator and that Creator was God (or Spirit) and, therefore, It could not create a material body. He also knew the Book of Genesis. If God did not create it . . . it was not made. So, if God did not create a material body . . . there is no material body. If God is Infinite Spirit and made this world in Its own image and likeness, then the body that God made must be Spirit . . . it must be spiritual . . . it must partake of the nature and character of Spirit.

Had Jesus returned from the tomb without that body, He would not have proven Immortality. He would not have proven

God as the Substance of all form . . . as the Creator of the Universe out of Its own Being. Since God is individual Being and God is your Mind and your Life . . . God is the Substance of your body, and your body is as Infinite and Eternal and Omnipresent as the Body of God . . . as the Substance or Life of God.

The moment you accept that fact intellectually, you begin ultimately to discern it spiritually and then you will demonstrate that the body has no power to age . . . lose its vitality . . . or die. Your body becomes as immortal as your own idea of Truth. If you acknowledge, "I am the Truth," you must also acknowledge, "My body is the Body of the Truth."

Scripture says your body is the Temple of God:

*What! Know ye not that your body is the temple of the Holy Ghost which is in you, which ye have of God, and ye are not your own!*

1 Corinthians 6:19

We are not judging by appearances . . . we are recognizing Truth as it is. The Truth is that God is The Substance of which this world was formed. Whether the world appears as earth, trees, sky, sun, moon, stars, or whether it appears as your body, it still is of the Substance and of the Activity of God, and it is Infinite . . . Immortal . . . Eternal . . . Omnipresent.

If God cannot change, neither can the body change. If God cannot age, neither can God, appearing as Body, age. Therefore, the body IS immortal and eternal and unless you understand that from the resurrection of the Master, you have lost the main point. There are reasons why it is necessary that we understand this.

It is senseless for us to go on as Infinite Way students . . .

claiming to know something and to have something . . . and yet continue being just as sick as other people, just as old as other people and just as decrepit as other people.

It is simply nonsensical to be a student of The Infinite Way and to CLAIM an understanding and demonstration of Truth, and yet to keep on experiencing the same diseases, the same accidents and the same everything else that other people have.

We are told to come out and be separate and we MUST come out and be separate . . . NOT in just claiming that we have demonstrated the fullness of the Christ-head . . . NO . . . but at least in claiming a progressive unfoldment of Christhood. It is only by constant application of effort toward the goal that we can show forth a little more of the Christ from year to year . . . not only in our loving kindness or understanding to each other . . . not only in our greater charity to each other . . . but also in our physical appearance.

Why should we claim that each year we are more loving . . . more kind . . . more just . . . and yet insist that each year we are older . . . weaker? It is not consistent.

It IS necessary that, through our Infinite Way study, we understand God as Love and, therefore, that we MUST show forth more love . . . more justice . . . more kindness . . . more peace toward each other. This is true . . . but . . . let us not stop there and separate the body from our spiritual demonstration. Let us bring the body into line WITH our spiritual demonstration and let us show forth more of the God-body each year. Let us show forth a higher concept of the real body so that we can bring our whole demonstration into line.

This point naturally follows: There is not a spiritual universe and a material universe. There is not something good in the world and something bad in the world. There is only

ONE Power and there is only ONE Presence and It is ALL
Good.

What we are called upon to do is change our concepts . . .
not change the world. You cannot change your body . . . even
by dying . . . but you can change the APPEARANCE of your
body by changing your concept OF your body. Your body cannot change. It is Spiritual . . . Infinite . . . Eternal . . . Harmonious . . . Perfect.

Going around affirming this statement won't help you one
bit . . . and it won't make it so . . . IT IS ALREADY SO. You
must come into the realization of it THROUGH knowing
WHY it is true.

God is individual Being. Therefore, God must be the Substance of individual Being and Body. God is the very Activity
of your Body. How can it be less Active tomorrow than today
or yesterday . . . if God is the Activity of It?

If God is the Activity of your Supply, how can your supply
be greater one day than another? The fluctuations in supply
are merely the result of the belief that you have a supply of
your own which can go up and down.

The fluctuations in the health and strength of the body
come only from the belief that we have a health or a body of
our own . . . instead of realizing GOD as individual Being . . .
GOD as the Substance of Being and of Body . . . and THEN
realizing that the ONLY capacity we have is God-capacity.
This capacity is not only a God-capacity for expressing Gratitude but it is also a God-capacity for expressing Youth . . .
Health . . . Vitality . . . Strength . . . Wisdom . . . and all the
other qualities of God.

You must come to the realization that this is NOT a partly
spiritual universe and partly material universe.

You must come to the realization that this universe is wholly spiritual and that there is no evil in it . . . therefore, it is useless to try to fight error or fight evil. Rather, agree with your adversary by saying, "All right . . . you may appear to be so but I am not going to fight it. I take my stand that God IS individual Being and, therefore, NOTHING can enter individual Being that defileth or maketh a lie."

If, temporarily, there is an appearance to the contrary, forget the appearance . . . overlook it . . . disregard it . . . and HOLD STEADFAST to the Truth that God IS individual Being. You have no life apart from God . . . no mind . . . no soul . . . no body . . . no CAPACITY apart from God. God is the Infinite Capacity of your Being and of your Body.

Meditate on that.

Nothing you can do or think can MAKE this true. It IS true . . . and it is not MADE true by any effort.

*Not by might, nor by power, but by my spirit, saith the Lord of hosts.*
                                                    Zechariah 4:6

As we open our consciousness to let GOD reveal this to us, instead of trying to argue it out or reason it out or find reasons why it cannot be or is not, let us forget that battle (the physical battle . . . or the mental battle) and realize this:

WHATEVER IS TRUE WILL REVEAL ITSELF TO YOU FROM WITHIN YOUR OWN BEING IF YOU WILL JUST OPEN YOUR CONSCIOUSNESS TO IT.

If there were a word not true in this, you would be informed of that, too.

Do NOT make a MENTAL effort to understand all this. It is far too deep for the mind to grasp. It is far too high for any

HUMAN intellect to agree with. It is too high spiritually. You will only be able to understand it through the Soul faculties. . . through your spiritual consciousness.

Therefore, open your mind in this wise . . . that whatever Truth IS, must reveal Itself to you . . . not by might . . . not by power . . . but by "MY SPIRIT" . . . for so saith the Lord.

ALOHA

# I Am the Vine

SOMEWHERE BACK IN THE DAYS of our old theological belief, we were under the impression that God's goodness to us depended upon our being worthy or deserving, and that if we were bad or had sinned, God withheld our good. If anything should be clear to those on the Spiritual Path it is this: God is LOVE, God is LAW, God is PRINCIPLE, God is DIVINE INTELLIGENCE, and God is ETERNAL LIFE.

If life were dependent upon our virtue, and our badness could interfere with life, or if anything at all could touch the harmonious flow of life, what would become of the Scriptural teaching that life is eternal and immortal? Does it say anything about life being immortal IF, WHEN AND AS YOU DO CERTAIN THINGS? NO! That would make immortal life dependent upon you or me, and it is not. Immortal life is dependent upon GOD, and there is nothing we can do to earn it, and there is nothing we can do to cause God to withhold it. We cannot pray to God to give us life, and there is no sin that can prevent the immortality and eternality of life.

GOD IS LOVE. What, then, could you or I do to change the nature of God? Could your own child do anything that would change YOUR love for him? No, of course not, and if, from the human standpoint, we are able to give love to our children often when they do not deserve it, HOW MUCH MORE LOVE is pouring forth from our Heavenly Father!

Can you accept the fact that GOD IS LOVE, not God is Love if you behave in a certain way, or not just when you are worthy and deserving? Can you accept the fact that GOD IS LOVE, and that God's rain falls on the just and the unjust alike? Did the Master, Christ Jesus, withhold good or healing because somebody was a sinner? Did He at any time ask the multitudes if they were good or if they squandered their money or saved it? In raising the dead did He ask if that person had been moral or immoral, honest or dishonest? Or did He, in beholding what the world calls death, destroy all belief in it by raising the individual to life? We all know the answer to that. At no time in His minstry did Jesus withhold healing, supply, forgiveness, restoration or reformation because of anyone's unworthiness or temporary sense of evil.

The principle is this: since GOD IS LOVE, our good must be finite without any ifs, ands, or buts, because God's Grace is not dependent upon something that you or I do or do not do. The Grace of God cannot be withheld. We can turn on or off the electricity and we can turn on or off the water, but we cannot start or stop the flow of God. GOD IS, AND GOD IS LOVE in Its completeness and fullness.

Let us now consider GOD IS LIFE. This does not mean that God is life at the age of six years or at sixteen. GOD IS LIFE. Then why is this not so at sixty, ninety, and a hundred and twenty? The reason is that the words I, me, and you enter the picture, and we say MY life or YOUR life, and immediately we think of the date on a birth certificate. If God is Life, of what consequence is the date on a birth certificate? God is the ONLY life and that life is infinite. Is it God's fault then if we change or get old or become sick and weak and decrepit? The life of God is infinite, eternal and immortal, and as that is the only life, we can forget MY age and YOUR age.

In the same way, GOD IS LOVE, so let us forget your conduct and my conduct. Some of us may be pretty bad today, some better, some worse. Perhaps some of us were better last year than we are this year, but the love of God for His Children has not changed, nor has the power of God been stilled. The right arm of God is mighty, the hand of God is not shortened. GOD IS POWER, but God being Good—GOD IS GOOD POWER. Can God then withhold help, supply or peace from any one? No, but you and I can block it by bringing in the words I, me, and you. "I" may not be deserving, or "I" may not be ready or have enough understanding, but it is not DEPENDENT upon my understanding.

As you go into the healing work the first calls will be for what the world calls "lesser claims" and in a short time you may begin to think, "Oh, I have some understanding," or "I am getting results through my understanding." If you DO you will never become a successful practitioner or teacher, because you will NEVER heal through YOUR understanding. God forbid that God's Presence and Power should be dependent upon MY understanding!

Healing is an activity of the Christ. Healing is an activity of GOD'S understanding. We have been saying MY life, MY health, MY supply, MY worthiness, MY understanding, and that is not involved at all—IT IS GOD'S UNDERSTANDING. The Master made that very clear when he said that of His own self He could do nothing, it is the Father within; therefore it is the FATHER'S UNDERSTANDING. The moment we open our consciousness to the flow of God and stop all this nonsense about OUR understanding and OUR good or bad behavior, we can be assured of this: the flow of God will erase and purify whatever of error is in our thought today, and will wipe out all penalty of past infraction. We must come into the realization that it is not our understanding that does this, but God's, and we MUST come out from the old Judaic ideas and beliefs of a God of punishment and reward. God is NOT a God of punishment and reward. GOD IS LOVE. GOD IS LIFE.

Every one of us still has some idea of God carried over from our childhood beliefs under orthodox and theological teachings, that we can gain God's favor by certain acts of omission or commission. Many still believe that God's favor can be gained by certain forms of prayer or worship, or self-restraint. This is not true. Of this we must be sure: GOD IS NOT INFLU-ENCED by man; that is, God is not influenced by individual you and me. GOD IS THE LIGHT, and if we walk out we will be in the light. God's rain falls, and if we want it WE must walk out into the rain. GOD IS, AND GOD IS LOVE. God is pouring forth Its INFINITE GRACE, and we are not accepting it because of the use of such words as I, me, and mine.

We must drop this belief that we play a part in obtaining God's Love, God's Grace, God's Givingness, and remember that the only part we play is to accept it by opening our consciousness to receive it.

The Writings of The Infinite Way contain hundreds of truths, but actually there is only ONE TRUTH that we must know. This one truth is THE NATURE OF GOD. Take this one thought into meditation: What is God? What is the nature of God? What is the character of God? What are the qualities of God? What is the true God?—not the God we were taught to worship as children, or that we ignorantly worship. Try to empty the already too full vessels, because they cannot be filled with the new wine. Empty your old misconceptions and be willing to begin all over, even if you are seventy, with the admission that you do not know God or you would be showing forth more of God's Grace. Forget all that you have thought or been taught about God and start afresh with this question, "What is God?" The moment you begin to realize that God is LOVE you will know that that love is flowing, unfettered, unlimited and free, because the nature of God is Infinity.

It would be impossible for God to hand us just a thimbleful of love; it would be impossible for God to give us ninety percent health, and it would be impossible for God to issue us sixty, seventy or eighty years of life. It is true that we are only DEMONSTRATING a thimbleful of love and supply, and just sixty, seventy or eighty years of life and strength. It may be perfectly true that there is not much love coming in or going out from us, but that has nothing to do with God. It has to do with some false belief that WE in some way, if only we can find the magic formula, can START GOD'S GOOD FLOWING, or that for some reason we have STOPPED God's Good. Is it not rather fantastic to believe that we should live only sixty, seventy or eighty years in good health and strength when the only life we have is God, and God's life is infinite and is not dependent upon what WE do about it? Life is dependent upon God's ability to maintain Its own life immortally, eternally and indefinitely.

Is it not strange that many have so few of the comforts of life when the Master told us that TRUTH IS THE COMFORTER? He did not say a LIMITED AMOUNT of comfort shall I send you, but He said THE COMFORTER—THE ONE, THE WHOLENESS OF THE COMFORTER, and all this time we have been satisfied with a small portion because we have believed that is all we have earned or deserved.

In making your will you should not ask how much each of your children deserves and say, "This one has been fairly good, so we will leave him a fair amount, and this one wasn't very good at all, we will cut him out, but this one has been very good so we will leave him a large amount." No. You should say, "We have three children and we will divide equally between them." How much more bountiful is our Heavenly Father, and HOW MUCH LESS DOES THE FATHER JUDGE THAN WE DO! God is not sitting in judgment or condemnation because of our sins, because the only reason behind our sins, faults and errors is ignorance.

Are we responsible for our ignorance? No. We have listened first to this one and then another, and through a feeling of obedience and loyalty and fear WE HAVE ACCEPTED THESE FALSE BELIEFS, but we are not punished for them.

The School of Life is open to any of us at any time we wish to begin, AND IN OUR ENLIGHTENMENT WE WILL FIND FREEDOM. It is only in ignorance that we find discord, limitation, sin, disease and death. In our ENLIGHTENMENT We find infinite abundance, freedom, immortality, eternality, so regardless of what your age may be, remember that there is only one subject on which you need to be enlightened: WHAT IS THE NATURE OF GOD?

"God is light, and in him is no darkness at all." Can you see God as the GREAT LOVE OF THE UNIVERSE in whom is no hate, envy, jealousy, malice, revenge, or even remembrance of the past? Can you see God as IMMORTAL, ETERNAL AND INFINITE LIFE? If so, you can bring harmony into your bodies and lives overnight. It is only the belief that YOU are or are not doing something that is causing sickness and sin in the flesh. It is only the BELIEF that the error lies within you, AND IT DOES NOT. So please try to remember this truth: MAN CAN NEVER INFLUENCE GOD. God is all good, and God's Grace endureth forever.

Eliminate the use of I, me, mine, and center your thought wholly on the word GOD. No longer think about "what am I in relationship to God?" Ask yourself these questions: Is God withholding any good? Can God withhold? Is there any reason for God to withhold? Does God have the power to shut off Its own benevolence, love, protection and care? There is no one on this earth great enough to make God do more than God Itself is doing, and no sin great enough to stop God from being God.

In the fifteenth chapter of John, we read:

*I am the true vine, and my Father is the husband-man.*

*Every branch in me that beareth not fruit he taketh away: and every branch that beareth fruit, he purgeth it, that it may bring forth more fruit.*

*Now ye are clean through the word which I have spoken unto you.*

*Abide in me, and I in you. As the branch cannot bear fruit of itself, except it abide in the vine; no more can ye, except ye abide in me.*

*I am the vine, ye are the branches: He that abideth in me, and I in him, the same bringeth forth much fruit: for without me ye can do nothing.*

*If a man abide not in me, he is cast forth as a branch, and is withered; and men gather them, and cast them into the fire, and they are burned.*

*If ye abide in me, and my words abide in you, ye shall ask what ye will, and it shall be done unto you.*

*Herein is my Father glorified, that ye bear much fruit; so shall ye be my disciples. As the Father hath loved me, so have I loved you: continue ye in my love.*

*If ye keep my commandments, ye shall abide in my love; even as I have kept my Father's commandments, and abide in his love.*

*These things have I spoken unto you, that my joy might remain in you, and that your joy might be full.*

*This is my commandment, That ye love one another, as I have loved you.*

Now we will go back to the first verse: "I am the TRUE vine and my Father is the husbandman" and "Ye are the branches." In your mind's eye, visualize a tree trunk from which grow many branches. Now, remove the trunk. All you have left are a lot of loose branches hanging in space, unconnected with each other and unconnected with any thing, each under the necessity of supporting itself up there in the air. This is, of course, an impossibility, and in a short time each of these branches will have used up the little life that was in itself and fallen away.

Now, let us restore the trunk of the tree and notice what has happened to the branches. We find them all connected with the tree, and the tree itself is ROOTED AND GROUNDED in the earth, from which IT IS DRAWING INTO ITSELF all the elements of the earth. FROM this great earth in which the tree is rooted, the moisture, the sunshine, the substance and minerals of the earth are being drawn into the tree, and all that is necessary for growth and development is flowing into the branches.

"I [Christ] am the true vine, and my Father is the Husbandman." The Christ is the vine (or the trunk) and WE are the branches. Each individual seems to be a branch all by himself, unconnected, separate and apart from every other branch, and each is probably wondering how he can get along by himself. Where does he get his life, wisdom and supply? What supports him? Each one is hustling along, struggling and striving by his own individual efforts for happiness and salvation, as if that struggle would maintain and sustain his life. And here the Scriptures clearly state that WE ARE BRANCHES BUT WE ARE CONNECTED WITH THE VINE. The Christ is that vine, so although invisible to human sense, each branch is connected with every other branch. None of us is separate and apart from each other, because we are all connected with the vine. We call that the Christ, the Invisible Spirit of God, or the Invisible Son of God, and each one of us is connected to each other because of this central vine or trunk. Now we find we are less dependent upon our OWN power and strength and wisdom because we are connected with this central vine.

Because of this vine there is no need for us to live off each other, or to struggle and fight against each other. WE ARE UNITED IN THE VINE—WE ARE ONE IN CHRIST.

We are one in Christ, but we go a step further and learn that MY FATHER IS THE HUSBANDMAN. God, the Universal Truth, the Universal Life, the Divine Mind, the Infinite Love, is the husbandman, or the equivalent of the earth in which the tree is rooted and grounded. We are branches invisibly connected to the vine, which in its turn is at one with God. "I and my Father are one." ". . . the Father is in me, and I in him" and so this invisible Christ, the invisible trunk of the tree or the vine rooted and grounded in God RECEIVES ALL OF THE GOOD INTO IT AND POURS IT OUT INTO US. Do you not see that our supply is not dependent upon us, any more than the supply of the branch of the tree is dependent upon

ITSELF? The branch is dependent only upon its CONTACT with the vine, and the vine's contact with the ground, the husbandman, or the Father within.

In our experience this principle operates something like this: as a student you are a branch, and when you go to a teacher or a practitioner, he may temporarily be the vine, the Christ—only, however, IF the teacher knows that of himself he is nothing but that vine. God, the Father within, is the husbandman, and the teacher is one with the husbandman. In his oneness with God, the husbandman, all the truth, the healing and supplying power, FLOWS FROM THE FATHER, THROUGH HIM, to you.

It was through this realization that the Master was able to feed and heal the multitudes, and through this same realization any teacher or practitioner can be the avenue through which Good flows to you. Is it dependent upon you? No. Is it dependent upon the practitioner or the teacher? No. It is dependent upon GOD'S GRACE FLOWING THROUGH THE VINE INTO THE BRANCHES, and as long as the vine remains rooted and grounded in God, just that long is God flowing through the vine unto you.

Please remember that you will not always need a teacher or practitioner to be your vine. That is only a temporary relationship. The Master told His disciples ". . . if I go not away, the Comforter will not come unto you. . . ." In other words, AFTER this truth has been demonstrated by contact with a teacher or practitioner, and after you have gained wisdom in the realization that the healing did not come FROM him but merely THROUGH him, from the Father within, you are ready for the next step.

It is then that you will realize, "The Invisible Christ, the vine, is not necessarily a person, not even a Jesus, but the

Christ is the very invisible part of ME. Therefore, I, as the branch, am connected with this invisible part of me, and it in turn is rooted and grounded in God. IT is the Son of God in me. So, the Christ is in the Father, and the Father is in me." That realization is the healing Truth.

At this point you may be wondering if there is anything you might do or not do that would stop this flow of Good. Yes, there is one thing. You can FORGET that there is an invisible vine to which you are connected. You can FORGET that the Father is the husbandman, and that all of God's good is flowing forth. You can begin to believe that I am separate and apart from you or that you are separate and apart from me, and that if you withhold something from me you will benefit. "I am the vine, ye are the branches; He that abideth in me, and I in him, the same bringeth forth much fruit: for without me ye can do nothing." UNLESS YOU RECOGNIZE YOUR CONSCIOUS ONENESS WITH THE INVISIBLE VINE, THE SON OF GOD OF YOU, YOU CAN DO NOTHING. You will be purged, and you will be a branch using up its little old threescore years and ten of life, and finally you will dry up and fall off. You are purged, NOT by God, but because "ye did not abide in ME and let MY word abide in you."

The moment you set yourself apart as a branch and forget your union with the Invisible Christ, just because you cannot see, hear, taste, touch or smell it and so decide you do not have it—"O ye of little faith"—you will be purged. Always remember, even in your direst troubles, in your worst diseases, or in your most dreadful sin, THAT YOU ARE STILL CONNECTED WITH THIS INVISIBLE VINE, AND THAT IT IN TURN IS ROOTED AND GROUNDED IN THE WHOLE OF THE FATHER, THE WHOLE OF THE HUSBANDMAN. The very nature of God prevents God from withholding Its flow

into the vine and through the vine into you and me. "If ye
abide in me, and my words abide in you, ye shall ask what ye
will, and it shall be done unto you." But that does not mean
that you are to ask in the sense of "Give me a more beautiful
home and a better automobile." No, no, no. You merely have
to ask what you will, ask for the continuance of Infinite
Grace, ASK FOR THE CONTINUOUS REALIZATION OF
OMNIPRESENCE.

"Ye ask, and receive not, because ye ask amiss. . . ." God
is Spirit and one does not ask Spirit for material things, which
is just what we do when we pray for THINGS, and then wonder
why they are not received. It is then that someone might say,
"Well, you don't go to church very often, and you aren't very
kind or forgiving, and you don't have your dishes washed by
noon, so you really are not very deserving."

GOD IS THE INFINITE FATHER. Think to what degree
you are a father or mother, and then think of God as INFINITE
Father. God is Infinite Father, no respecter of persons, and
through the invisible vine is continuously filling us with everything necessary for our unfoldment. "Herein is my Father glorified, that ye bear much fruit. . . ." Do you understand the
meaning of that? Your father is glorified ONLY in proportion
as you bear much fruit, rich fruit. Your Father is not glorified
by penny-pinching, or by going into a market asking for the
cheapest cuts of meat and the cheapest products. Your Father
is not glorified when you have to get along with a third-hand
automobile. No, no, no, that does not glorify the Father.

The Father does not require that you have anything in the
material realm, but WHAT YOU DO HAVE OF GOOD IS BUT
THE EVIDENCE OF THE FATHER'S GLORY AND NOT
YOURS. If you do have a good home or a good income and
begin to believe that you are responsible for them because of

YOUR understanding or YOUR personal goodness, be not surprised if you are cut off from them. That would be because you were glorifying your OWN qualities, your OWN nature and character, and those you do not possess. "Why callest thou me good? None is good, save one, that is God," and when you realize, "THE GLORY OF GOD IS SHOWING FORTH THROUGH THIS GOOD THAT HAS COME TO ME," you may expect even greater fruitage BECAUSE YOU HAVE ACKNOWLEDGED THE SOURCE. "In all thy ways acknowledge HIM" and He will give you unlimited and abundant good. "IF ye keep my commandments, ye shall abide in my love."

The Master gave us only two commandments: one was to love God, and the other was to love your neighbor as yourself, and so HOW can you love God except in the realization of God as Love? How can you love God if you believe that He is withholding some good or is punishing you, or doing something that you would not do to your own children? You can only love and honor God if you can see Him as GLORIOUS, INFINITE LIFE—LIFE UNFETTERED, UNHINDERED AND UNAFFECTED BY MAN'S VIRTUE OR TRANSGRESSION. To love God and your neighbor as yourself is to visualize that tree and remember that every branch is your neighbor and that your neighbor is deriving his good THROUGH THE SAME INVISIBLE CHRIST FROM THE FATHER, THE HUSBANDMAN.

It may be necessary occasionally, even while you voice this prayer for your neighbor, that you temporarily lend or give him some of the world's goods in order to help him over an acute stage of lack or limitation, but you will never have to undertake to continuously uphold or support the deserving poor, BECAUSE THERE WILL BE NO DESERVING POOR IF YOU LOVE YOUR NEIGHBOR AS YOURSELF. Every time you see an individual in some form of sin, disease, lack, limitation, deformity, or even death, just catch a glimpse of our tree and silently realize, "Thank God for that trunk." That trunk unites us in oneness and enables each of us to draw from the one Infinite Source, and not from each other. It is then that you are loving God supremely and your neighbor as yourself, because you are knowing the same TRUTH about your neighbor that you are knowing about yourself.

The Master was careful to describe 'neighbor' so we would not make any mistake. Your enemy is your neighbor. When you pray for your neighbor, be sure to include your enemy, for unless you pray for them that persecute you and despitefully use you, and forgive them until seventy times seven, you are just loving CERTAIN neighbors, and people have gotten into a lot of trouble for that.

"Greater love hath no man than this, that a man lay down his life for his friends." We lay down our life every time we declare, "I have no life—God is MY life and God is YOUR life." God is the ONLY life, the ONLY love, the ONLY substance, and the ONLY supply. Every time you reach out to Truth someone is laying down his personal sense of life in the realization that his life, being God's life, is YOUR life. Your life, being God's life, is HIS life, and it is ONE LIFE. So, when we give up that personal sense of life and say, "This is not my life, this is the life of GOD, which is mine," we automatically say goodbye to a sixty- or seventy-year span and are resurrected in the REALIZATION OF GOD AS THE INFINITY OF OUR LIFE.

In these passages from John we catch the true vision of God, the Infinite Invisible, as the source of all good, which can in no wise withhold any good. Good is forever pouring Itself forth individually in what we call the Son of God, the

Christ, which is the invisible part of you, and then through that invisible you out into the physical body, out into the mind and Soul and Spirit of individual being TO SHOW FORTH THE GLORY OF GOD. We are warned, the branch CANNOT bear fruit of itself, so there can be no personal goodness, health or wealth. The branch must draw it THROUGH the vine FROM the God-head.

"Every branch in me that beareth not fruit he taketh away" might lead us to believe that after all God probably punishes a little bit, but that is not true. IF YOU DO NOT ABIDE IN THIS TRUTH, if you do not maintain your conscious oneness with the Christ WITHIN YOU, and THROUGH IT your oneness with the Father, you will be purged. It will be YOU separating yourself from God's Grace, and thus being purged, destroyed, burned up, withered away. To ABIDE in this truth is to live and move and have your BEING in this consciousness of your oneness with the Christ, and the Christ's oneness with the Father.

This, of course, does not mean that we are connected with people, but connected with the Invisible, so that were you set down in mid-ocean or in the desert, you would be able to say, "Ah, but I am STILL a branch of the vine, and the vine is STILL connected with the husbandman, God, and therefore the place whereon I stand is Holy Ground." Every time we think thoughts of hopelessness and despair it is as if we acknowledge that we are a branch cut off from the vine, and the vine from the husbandman, and that we cannot reach either; yet all the time It is right here where we are. IT is within you, and IT is connected with OMNIPRESENCE.

"I go to prepare a place for you . . . that where I am, there ye may be also." You may be wondering "Where is I AM?" Wherever you are saying "I AM," that is where I am; and where

I AM, that is where you are. Wherever you are there is the vine, and the Father, the Husbandman—the Father, the Son, and the Holy Ghost.

You must always remember that the Husbandman, God, does not give and does not withhold—IT JUST CONTINUALLY IS. The vine of you, the Christ, is not sitting in judgment, but is here to bless and to forgive, to supply and to love. What was the mission of the Master? "Go and show John again those things which ye do hear and see; the blind receive their sight, and the lame walk, the lepers are cleansed and the deaf hear, the dead are raised up, and the poor have the gospel preached to them." The Christ is there to support, supply, maintain, sustain, to heal, to forgive and regenerate. It is here to resurrect from the grave and TO BRING ABOUT THE ASCENSION.

There is no word in the entire message and mission of the Master that gives any reason for self-condemnation. "Neither do I condemn thee: go, and sin no more." If you return to the old material state of consciousness and do not abide in the word, you will be purged again and again. Every time you forget that you are a branch connected with the invisible vine, which in its turn is connected with the husbandman, the Father within, you are committing a sin. You can be a prodigal twelve times if you wish, but YOU will pay the penalty.

If you go back to the belief of a selfhood separate and apart from God—a branch hanging in space—you will bring upon yourself lack and limitation of supply, health, strength and eternality, but "if ye abide in me, and my words abide in you, ye shall ask what ye will, and it shall be done unto you. Herein is my Father glorified, that ye bear much fruit . . . so shall ye be my disciples."

# The Deep Silence of My Peace

"My peace I give unto you: not as the world giveth, give I unto you," but *My peace*, a peace to which you must cling even when the turmoil which disturbs the outer world comes into your world to bring about either doubt or fear of those things or conditions that exist in the world.

If you really want to attain a sense of peace, learn to drop all thought or concern for whatever it is that is disturbing in the outer picture. Now, it is not easy for me to write this any more than it is easy for you to read it, but the desire in the hearts of most of us right now is for some solution to an outer problem, a problem of human existence, to something that is disturbing us in the world of health or wealth. Most of us are concerned about something in our human affairs, and we are seeking a solution to it. There is nothing wrong with that; the solution must appear because harmony must appear, but we will fail to find the solution as long as we are concerned with the problem and the solution of the problem.

We can have the answer to that problem here and now if we can sufficiently drop our concern for it in the realization of this "My peace," that is, the Christ-peace. This is Jesus speaking: "My peace I give unto you: not as the world giveth" —not the peace of physical health or material wealth, not the satisfaction of personal desires, but something far transcending these, something that, when we experience it, wipes out entirely the need for human demonstration. That is what we want to achieve here and now. Right now we must, and many of us can, drop this concern, lose concern for whatever it is, whatever the nature of it may be, that we brought with us when we turned to these words. We cannot do this humanly by telling it to get out or "get . . . behind me, Satan," but we can open our consciousness at this minute to a realization of "My peace."

Watch this as it flows through your consciousness; watch as you open yourself, even with the question: "What is this 'My peace'? What is the spiritual nature of peace? What is the spiritual nature of harmony?" You will remember that in order to be that man whose being is in Christ, we must come to the end of the road of seeking and searching and come to some measure of awareness that we have already arrived. In order to do that, we relax from every sense of desire for achievement or desire for demonstration in the feeling that the presence of God dissolves all false appearances.

The presence of God is a "peace, be still" to every type of storm. There are more storms than ever were on the seas; there are more storms in our thought than on all the oceans; but the Christ is a "peace, be still" to every kind of storm, to every form of discord, to every nature of inharmony. "Peace, be still. . . . My peace"—*My* peace, the Christ-peace, "the peace that passeth understanding," is the peace that comes with the realization:

> *"I will never leave thee, nor forsake thee." If you walk through the water, I will be with you. "Whither thou goest, I will go . . . thy people shall be my people." Never—"I will never leave thee, nor forsake thee." Whithersoever thou goest, I will go. Yea, though you walk through the valley of the shadow of death, I will walk with you. I will be with you, I will be in you, and I will be through you. Fear not, fear not, I am with you.*

From the depth of this inner silence come forth the healing waters. These waters bring everlasting life. Out of the depth of this silence comes the Spirit, which appears as our cloud by day and our pillar of fire by night. Out of the depth of this silence come the safety and the security which always follow the peace that God gives.

The reason for peace is that there is nothing to fear. While there is something to fear, there is no peace. Once the peace has descended upon us, the prayer is complete; the reason for disturbance, for sickness, for lack has gone. The *feeling* of peace is the successful prayer. There is no successful communion until "the peace that passeth understanding" descends upon us.

All prayer, all communion with God, is only for one purpose—not to make any kind of demonstration, but to achieve for us this sense of peace, or well-being, this realization: "Lo, I am with you until the end of time. Lo, I am always with you." Let us have that sense of the divine Presence, and we shall have the answered prayer. Let us fail to achieve this sense of peace, and the prayer is not a prayer. In "My presence" the fire does not burn, the water does not drown; in "My presence" the storms do not rage. The power of Christ is the answer to every form of inharmony. The *feeling* of the Presence is in itself a prayer. Let us understand this: Our problem is at an end—not when we think we have found a solution, but when we have *felt* this inner peace.

There is a bond between all of us, the bond that holds us together at this moment. That bond is the love of God. That love of God is our mutual at-one-ment. It makes us at-one with God and at-one with each other, so that the flow of God to, and through, any one of us is instantaneously the flow of God through everyone within range of our being. "One with God is a majority," and because we are one with God and one with each other, all that the Father has is showing forth, is manifesting as our individual experience, the individual experience of each one of us. Whatever is true spiritually of one of us in demonstration is now true of all of us because of our oneness with each other through our oneness in God, so the "peace, be still" that is of God, that touches the Soul of one of us, touches the Soul of all of us.

The solution of the outer problem is automatically taken care of in the realization of this inner peace. The peace within produces harmony and joy without. The activity of Christ within results in the stilling of the waves without. The "peace, be still" within appears as the daily manna without. The realization of this divine Presence, this feeling of divine Love through us, is the temple of God in which we live and move and have our being—even when we are out in the world. The word of God is our abiding place. Even when we move in and out of this world, we are abiding in this Word if we feel this divine Presence.

*I will never leave you, nor forsake you, but you
must abide in Me; you must abide in My word. I will
never leave you, nor forsake you. I will be with you,
whithersoever thou goest, but you must turn within
to Me; you must make Me your abiding place; you
must take My word into your mouth, into your consciousness. You must take the remembrance of My
presence with you wherever you go. I will never leave
you, nor forsake you, but be sure that you do not leave
the Word out of your mouth.*

Recognize the divine Presence in the heart and Soul of all
those you meet, friend or foe. Recognize that the individual
Soul is the abiding place of God. That the world itself does not
know it is of no concern to you or to me. They, too, will
awaken as we recognize God in the midst of them.

In this work that we are doing now I want to reveal to you
a principle of healing, of protecting, and of supplying; but a
principle that will operate without your taking thought, without your making statements, without your doing mental work,
and without your begging or pleading or beseeching God. I
would like to show you a principle of healing that operates
completely without what the metaphysical world calls treatment. In this teaching, you will find that the healing principle
is a state of peace, a state of peace that we achieve through
the realization of the Presence. That is our form of prayer—
just the realization of the Presence, just the *feeling* of a state of
peace.

We remain in communion until a sense of peace steals
over us, a sense of peace which comes from but one recognition:

*I am with you; I will never leave you, nor forsake you. I, in the midst of you, am mighty. My presence will go before you to make the crooked places straight. I will go before you to prepare a place for you. "My peace I give unto you: not as the world giveth"—not with human honors or human wealth, but a peace transcending man's understanding, a peace that comes when the Christ is enthroned in your consciousness as the source of your health and the source of your supply.*

No other peace can be lasting, except the peace that comes as the Christ is enthroned as the source of good and as the only power in individual experience.

*I live; yet not I, but Christ liveth my life. I can do all things through Christ. Christ is my strength; Christ is my redeemer, my saviour, Christ is the law of resurrection unto my body and unto my business; Christ is my bread and wine and water—not to be achieved, not to be earned. Christ never leaves me, nor forsakes Me. Therefore the bread and the water and the wine and the meat are always here within my being: I am with you and I am the bread of life. I am with you and I am the meat. I am with you and I am the wine and I am the water and I am the resurrection. I am life eternal and I, Life eternal, will never leave you, nor forsake you. My peace I give unto you.*

*No longer will you live by bread, but by My presence. My presence will be sufficient for you. You will no longer seek for anything except for Me, and you will know that in finding Me, the Christ, you will have found your peace, your security, your confidence, your*

*reward, your health, strength, and eternality. No longer
seek after the things of the world, otherwise you cannot
receive the peace that the world knows nothing of.
Seeking the things of the world, you find the peace that
the world can give you. Seeking the realization of my
Presence, you will find "the peace that passeth understanding."*

In this prayer the nature of the problem is of no importance
—only the realization of this peace, of this Presence. It will
take care of the problem regardless of its nature or its intensity
or of the length of its duration. "Though your sins be as scarlet, they shall be as white as snow"—in one instant.

*I will take you by a way; I will take you by a way
called the Christ, in which every thought, every need,
and every desire will be satisfied and fulfilled in the
realization of the Word; Christ is my fulfillment; Christ
is my saviour; Christ is the source and fount of all my
good. I shall look unto Christ, not unto man, but unto
Christ, unto this sense of peace within me. In the
realization of this peace, I have found the Christ, I have
realized the Christ. The Christ has become visible and
tangible.*

Sometimes in this meditation I see right before my closed
eyes a luminous crucifix, and it is the symbol of the crucifying
of our faith, belief, and dependence on anything external to
our own being. Right now, right here, we are crucifying our
own faith or dependence on a presence or power outside of
our own being. As we rise above the crucifying of our outer
dependence, we make the ascension into a state of consciousness in which, regardless of the storm, we close the eyes and
say: " 'Peace, be still.' *My* peace is with me."

Think now—that from the moment you have crucified your faith and dependence, your reliance on man and things, and have come into the realization that a state of peace within is life eternal and harmonious without, from that moment you have made the ascension from this world. And only then can you say with the Master: " 'I have overcome the world.' I have overcome the need for anything or anyone. I have found Christ within to be my salvation, my supplier, and my supply, my healer and my redeemer. I have found that the source of satisfaction is this realization of peace within. My fulfillment now is always from within. I have crossed out the belief that my help must come from without. I have crossed out the belief that anything or anyone external is necessary in the realization of my eternal harmony." All that has come about through the *feel* of a peace within, not due to anything without, but due to a divine Presence within. The divine Presence has always been there. *Now* when the storms threaten without, *now* when the waves dash against our ship, let us remember this experience.

It may take five minutes for the peace to descend; it may take fifteen minutes. There are obstinate beliefs in this world, but if we are patient and know what it is we are waiting for— the assurance from within—it will descend. That is all we are waiting for—the assurance from within. The prayer is not complete until the assurance comes from within: "Lo, I am with you alway . . . Fear not, I am with you."

How easy it is to rest in the deep Silence, to relax all cares. "Ah, yes," you say, "but when we return to the world, aren't the troubles still there?" No, not for you and not for me. A thousand may feel them at your left and ten thousand at your right, but they will not come nigh you as you dwell in this deep Silence.

It may take practice, but whenever agitation comes to your thought, find a place to rest and relax and wait for this peace to descend upon you. As this peace descends upon you inwardly, you may be sure, whatever the name or nature of the storm without, it also is being stilled.

Isn't it easy in this atmosphere to say, "Father, forgive them, they know not what they do"? All these disturbers of the world—isn't it easy to forgive them and to realize that they have disturbed only because of their ignorance of this peace, just as we were ignorant of it before we started this communion? Nothing that defileth or maketh a lie can enter the deep Silence. By this you can see that we are not disturbed by our own fears or doubts or problems. When we come into a sense of agitation, it is usually because we are disturbed by the world's fears and doubts and problems. We are merely receiving-stations for the world's troubles. If they were our troubles, they would still be troubling us. They never were our troubles, even when they reflected themselves in our affairs.

Those of you who feel this, who are touched by the divine Presence, will want to maintain it always. There is a way: It is the way of frequent silence and frequent meditation, frequent opening of thought to the Christ, to the realization of the divine Presence. At the first flurry of an entrance of the world into your consciousness, retire into this—even while at your work. "Be not afraid, it is I."

As a person, you no longer need to desire anything or to want anything or to acknowledge a need for anything. As a person, now, you can relax and be assured that there is a Presence in the midst of you, a Light, a Being, and Its function is to fulfill your entire experience, to fill it full of spiritual good. Its function in the midst of you is to know what things you have need of and to provide them. There is no need for you to acknowledge any lack. There is no need for you to acknowledge any need. The stillness, the silence, is God's abiding place. In the stillness and in the silence, God lives and expresses and fulfills and reveals and unfolds, and Its world appears to you in forms of harmony, grace, and beauty.

If you are as a little child, if you are relaxed, if you have given up the personal sense of "I" at this moment—if only for this moment—you come to the place where it is almost as if you were looking over your own shoulder and watching God appear, just as you might watch a sunset or a moonrise and yet not reach out and try to help, just quietly be a beholder. Sometimes when you see a beautiful flower, the first thought that comes into your mind is, "And a fool hath said in his heart there is no God." Have you ever looked at a beautiful flower or a mountain scene, sunrise or sunset, and had that thought flash right into your mind, "And a fool hath said in his heart there is no God"? That is because you knew that "only God can make a tree," as the poet has told us. You knew that only God could fashion such a sunset, create such a mountain setting. You knew that it was your joy and your pleasure and your privilege to behold God revealing Itself in these beautiful forms and colors. That is all you were doing; you were beholding God revealing Itself to you in these wondrous varieties of beauty and grace.

So in this moment of relaxed selfhood, in this silent communion, you know now that you can of your own self do nothing; it truly is the Father within you that doeth the works. In this moment of supreme stillness and silence, the human mind is not trying to make a demonstration; the human mind has gone even a step further and acknowledges no lack, no limitation, no need, but just feels:

*I am home in Thee. "I and my Father are one." I*
*rest in Thee. I feel "the peace that passeth understand-*
*ing." I know the glow of the divine Presence. He that*
*fashioned me shall preserve me. He shall be a light unto*
*my feet; He shall go to prepare a place for me, because*
*His is the kingdom and the power and the glory. This*
*is His kingdom, not mine. This is His power, not mine.*
*This is His glory, not mine. As if we of our own under-*
*standing or power have raised up this man! No, the God*
*of Abraham, the God of Isaac, the God of Jacob hath*
*done this thing. And if the Spirit of God dwell in us,*
*that same Spirit that raised up Jesus from the dead will*
*quicken also our mortal bodies.*

How can you know if the Spirit of God dwells in you? If
you can be relaxed, if you can be at peace, if you can rest, rest.
"In quietness and in confidence shall be your strength," not
in mental work, not in treatment. "In quietness and in confidence shall be your strength."

Be still and let me show you the Father's glory; let me
show you how the Father can come to you, revealing health,
revealing harmony, revealing peace—and all without your
doing a thing.

*"Not by might, nor by power, but by my spirit, saith*
*the Lord." I will not leave you comfortless. I will send*
*you a comforter—even the Spirit of Truth. And It will*
*be all things to you. Rest from your mental labors, rest*
*from your doubts and from your fears.*

No one ever fears who has tasted or touched God. "Yea,
though I walk through the valley of the shadow of death," I

will not fear. How could David fear, since he had already learned that "Thou art with me"? If, in this moment of still-ness and of silence, you feel even the tiniest touch of the Christ, you will never again fear, though you walk through the desert or through the wilderness or through the waters or through the flames or through the valley of the shadow of death. You will never again fear because the remembrance of this little Touch will be a reassurance:

> *Before Abraham was, I was right there with you. Lo, I am with you unto the end of the world, I will never leave you, nor forsake you. As I was with Abra-ham, so I will be with you. As I was with Moses in the Red Sea, in the wilderness, so I will be with you. Though the waters pass over you, they will not drown you.*

I do not ask you to believe the signs. I do not ask you to believe, even if you experience a healing; I will only ask you to believe if you feel the Touch within you, the Presence, the Light, the Life.

Remember, if your thoughts want to wander, that it is in quietness and in confidence that you find your peace, not in your mental wanderings, not in trying to fulfill some human need—but in quietness and in confidence.

When the Master says to us: "Ye shall know the truth, and the truth shall make you free," remember that the truth that you are to know is that "I in the midst of thee am mighty," that My peace is your salvation, that quietness and confidence is the prayer, that we do not attain our good by might or by power, but by a gentle Spirit. We are quiet as we accept God's grace. We let God's grace flow to us, through us, but remember: "Go and tell no man." Tell no one what things you have discovered; do not throw your pearls before the unprepared thought. These things that are whispered to you in silence will be shouted from the housetops as demonstration, not by your voice, not by rushing to tell your friend or neighbor, but by demonstration.

Be still, be still and know. But be *still* and know; do not do it aloud.

"Be *still*, and know."

# The Fourth
# Dimension of Life

When the Master, Christ Jesus, says, "I can of my own self do nothing, the Father within me doeth the works," when Paul says, "I live; yet not I, but Christ liveth in me"—they are revealing the Fourth Dimension of life in which you do not live "by bread alone," nor by personal will, effort or even personal wisdom.

There comes a point in your experience when you are not solely you—but in which you are conscious of a Presence within. This point of transition comes when the Presence becomes real within you and takes over your life. From the moment of this transitional experience you do not again take any anxious thought for your life because there is always this IT—this Christ—or divine Presence, and IT brings to you the harmonies of your daily experience.

In this transitional experience you pass from being merely a human being, thinking your own thoughts, planning your own life, arranging your own affairs to a place in Consciousness where you really and truly "feel" this inner Presence, and you then live as if you had stepped aside a little—say two or three inches to the side of yourself—and are watching your life being lived for you.

If you, at that moment, are in the business world, you will find business coming to you that you were not personally responsible for—that is, you had made no personal effort to secure. If you are an author or composer, you will find ideas flowing, such ideas as you have never dreamed of, flowing to you from within—and you will know that you are not creating them, but they are given you by an inner Grace.

If you are in Spiritual Work, the Healing or Teaching Ministry, you will find patients and students being led to you, and all will be spiritually healed and led by the Spirit. Thereby you would understand that "I live—yet not I, but Christ liveth my life. The Father worketh hitherto, and I work."

At this point you become the instrument for the operation and activity of divine Consciousness. When the Master says, "The Father within doeth the works" you will understand that He means that He—of His own powers, His own knowledge, wisdom or strength—does nothing, but rather that the activity of Truth in His Consciousness performs the miracles of healing, comforting and feeding the multitudes.

You, therefore, become the vehicle through which Life lives itself. You become the Messenger carrying the divine Message. You will know that you are now no longer living your life but that the Presence and Power is living it and you are its instrument, mode of expression or avenue of Its activity and of course you will now understand why the Master could say, "I and the Father are one but the Father is greater than I."

This is not duality or separation. This is not going back to the belief of God and man, since we have learned that God manifests Itself as individual you and me, but rather this reveals that I, God, being the infinite universal divine Principle in Life, appear as individual you and me so that truly, "I and the Father are one." The Inner manifests and expresses Itself as the outer individual.

These, however, are merely statements of truth until the moment of your transition, at which time they become Reality. In other words, there is an actual time in your life when these are no longer statements of Truth, when the Presence becomes an actual experience.

When you have attained that point in consciousness where Christ is living your life, you find that Christ is also maintaining and sustaining your entire existence; providing you with activity, intelligence, love and the necessary strength and health to carry on your work. It is also supplying all necessary finances, recognition, reward and compensation. The Infinite Invisible which now has taken over your life fulfills Itself in your experience. It comes to be the fulfillment of your life. It provides transportation, accommodations, opportunity and successful achievement.

Those engaged in the Spiritual Ministry quickly learn that It provides everything necessary to the fulfillment of the Message since "My doctrine is not mine, but His that sent me." Whatever is necessary for the expression of the Message, be assured of this, whoever is inspired as the Messenger is supported, maintained and sustained by That which is the Source and Inspiration of the Message.

Those engaged in business, arts, professions or home duties immediately feel the release from personal responsibility as It becomes the Soul and activity of their being.

Now you understand that when Jesus speaks of the Father within, He speaks of the divine Power and Presence that animated His being, and this was the healing power, the power that multiplied the loaves and fishes; the power that raised Lazarus from the dead. In the same way you understand that when Paul speaks of being able to do all things through Christ, he likewise is referring to the divine Power which we in *The Infinite Way* term the Infinite Invisible and that it was this Power that gave him his message and his mission to carry out to the world of his day. That Presence also provided his strength, his inspiration and his supply.

The "Father within me that doeth the works" of the Master, the "Christ which strengtheneth me" of Paul, is the same spirit of Truth, that same Consciousness of Truth that appeared as manna (as a "cloud by day and a pillar of fire by night") through Moses; as cakes baked on the stones, a raven bringing food, a widow sharing through Elijah; as the marvellous healing at the Temple Gate Beautiful through Peter and John. "The same Spirit that raised up Jesus Christ from the dead will quicken also your mortal bodies."

Do you see? *There is* a Spirit in you; there is a divine Spark which we call the Christ, which lifts you into the Fourth Dimension of life—into a state of Consciousness in which you do not live by personal efforts, personal will or wisdom, or even personal health—in which you find yourself empowered from within, from the Kingdom of your own being.

Again, I repeat, there is a point which you attain in this world where you realize that you do not live, but the Infinite Invisible is living your life. It goes before you to make all arrangements for you. It goes with you as the Source and activity of your daily life. It becomes manna, water, meat. It appears as protection, security and health. And should the temple of your body, business or home be destroyed, It will raise it up quickly. It will restore the years of the locusts.

Should you experience difficulties, discords, fears—it is only that through these trials and temptations the world may see that within you is the power of overcoming. "He that is within me is greater than he that is in the world."

Now, in this state of exalted Consciousness, in this Fourth Dimension which is Christ Consciousness, you go forward without material obstruction, without physical, mental, moral or financial hindrances; in that state of divine Consciousness which is Heaven, the realities of God's world are become so real that all sense of the three-dimensional world of limitation has faded out.

As you understand the timelessness of this Presence and Power, you will understand that regardless of when IT makes ITS appearance, it has always existed within you—not yet realized and achieved. In other words, this Infinite Invisible is with you now, but only through the development of Truth in your consciousness, only through the activity of Truth in your consciousness, will It become as real and powerful in your experience as it was in the Hebrew prophets and Christian seers of old.

Now let us give a moment to the nature or function of this Power we call the Christ. The Christ is the invisible activity, substance and law of all that appears as effect. It is for this reason you must not be hypnotized by appearances. By this I mean, if you are humanly healthy or wealthy, do not believe you have found immortality or security. If you have a bomb shelter or mountain cave, do not believe you have secured safety. Do not place your faith or dependence on anything, any effect, any person in the outer realm. On the other hand, do not fear sin, disease, or lack. There is no power in them. "Yea, though I walk through the valley of the shadow of death I will fear no evil, for *Thou art there.*"

When faced with human conditions of good or evil—this is the time to realize instantly that all harmonious spiritual effect is produced by the activity of the Christ. The activity of the Christ within you will maintain and sustain all happy and harmonious events and experiences, and should these be temporarily injured or destroyed, be not alarmed. Be not concerned for the organs or functions of your body or your financial or political structure, since the activity of the Christ is the law of Resurrection onto all of these.

The purpose of our Spiritual Ministry is to lead you into the Fourth Dimension, where you do not live by effect, you do not live by bread alone or vitamins or minerals—where you live by virtue of the activity of the Christ, the Infinite Invisible, and—in this Fourth Dimension of life, which is Spiritual Consciousness—all effect will appear in your experience as you have need of it, and it will appear abundantly.

Remember, however, that Christ is the foundation, the law or the continuity of your experience.

The Fourth Dimension is that state of consciousness in which your entire reliance, faith, dependence and understanding are in the Infinite Invisible, and in which you learn to enjoy the fruits of the Spirit, the harmonies of daily living by Grace.

While you will not behold this with your eyes, yet in the secret inner chamber of your being, in your meditation, you will spiritually discover the activity of the Christ in your life.

# Contemplative
# Meditation
# with Scripture

CONTEMPLATIVE MEDITATION is the preparatory step before pure meditation without words or thoughts, and its main purpose is to keep the mind stayed on God—to acknowledge Him in all our ways—so that in quietness and in confidence we may "be still, and know that I am God."[1]

We know that "the natural man receiveth not the things of the Spirit of God: for they are foolishness unto him: neither can he know them, because they are spiritually discerned."[2] Therefore, only in contemplative meditation, conscious of scriptural truth, can we prepare ourselves to attain our divine sonship or the Buddha mind. It is promised: "If ye abide in me, and my words abide in you, ye shall ask what ye will, and

[1] Psalm 46:10.
[2] 1 Corinthians 2:14.

it shall be done unto you."[3] In other words, if we abide in the Word and if we let the Word abide in us, we will bear fruit richly.

Thus contemplating truth, we attain the gift of discernment through which we attain that truth which the "natural man" cannot know. This is affirmed in the Bhagavad-Gita. "See Me! Thou canst not! nor, with human eyes, Arjuna! Therefore I give thee sense divine. Have other eyes, new light! And look! This is My glory unveiled to mortal sight!"[4]

To meditate properly—to develop the ability to practice meditation—it is necessary to understand certain spiritual principles of life. Unless a meditation has in it a conscious awareness of a spiritual principle, it will not be beneficial. It can in fact lead to just a mental stillness in which there is no spiritual fruitage or "signs following." Therefore, you must not only know why you are meditating, but you must know specific principles to take into your meditation.

Let us take the major principle of life upon which a harmonious existence can be experienced: I am *I*. Declare this to yourself, because it is indisputable. You are not someone else: you are yourself! "I am *I*." In the great lesson on supply taught in Chapter 17 of 1 Kings, when Elijah asked the poor widow to bring him a morsel of bread, she went and did according to his saying, even though she had but a handful of meal and a little oil in a cruse, "and she, and he, and her house, did eat many days." He did not inquire of her what she had or what she needed. His whole attitude was, "What do you *already* have in your house?"

Let us see how this can be applied in practical experience.

[3] John 15:7.
[4] *The Song Celestial*, trans. Sir Edwin Arnold (London: Routledge and Kegan Paul), p. 63.

When many of us are gathered together in spiritual awareness, it is easy to feel the peace among us. There is quietness and confidence, and certainly there is an absence of hate, bigotry, bias, or jealousy. Let us now ask ourselves this question: "How did this peace get here and how were bias, bigotry, and hatred eliminated?" The answer is clear. We brought into this atmosphere the peace that is here. Whatever stillness and confidence is present—whatever love is with us—we brought it. Whatever of hatred, jealousy, or discord is not here, we did not bring into our presence.

What have you in your house? What have you in your consciousness? You have love, you have life, you have cooperativeness and you have peace. What did you bring into this temple? This temple is the temple of God, but what made it so? Your being here in an atmosphere of love and mutuality. Then it is not that this room is the temple of God: it is that *you* are the temple of God! "Know ye not that ye are the temple of God?"[5] Ye are the temple of God *if* so be you left your personal feelings outside, *if* so be you left human limitations of anger, fear, and jealousy outside, *if* so be you brought in your consciousness the love and the peace we feel here. Because we *do* feel it, and because we are cognizant of the peace that is in our midst, we know beyond measure that you brought it. In other words the degree of peace, love, and joy we feel—the degree of healing consciousness that is with us —is the degree that you brought here in your consciousness.

There can be no greater degree of healing consciousness than that which you brought with you; there can be no greater degree of health than that which you brought with you; there can be no greater degree of supply than what you brought with you; and how much you brought with you depends on how

[5] 1 Corinthians 3:16.

much truth you know in your consciousness, what constitutes your consciousness, and who you are and what your true identity is.

The Master Christ Jesus asked: "Whom do men say that I am?" If the men are just human beings with no spiritual discernment, they will say that he is a Hebrew prophet, or a resurrected Hebrew prophet, or someone brought down from the human past. But "Whom say *ye* that I am?" and Peter replied: "Thou art the Christ, the Son of the living God."[6] When Peter answered the Master, he was revealing your true identity and mine, and when Christ Jesus said, "Call no man your father upon the earth: for one is your Father, which is in heaven,"[7] he was referring to your consciousness and my consciousness. As a matter of fact, his entire ministry was a revelation of man's spiritual *sonship*. Therefore, you can bring infinite peace, infinite harmony, infinite healing consciousness, and infinite supply into a group of people, but you can accomplish this in only one way, by knowing that "I and my Father are one,"[8] and "Son, thou art ever with me, and all that I have is thine."[9]

Think what would happen if you set aside ten minutes every morning to be separate and apart from the outside world for the purpose of contemplating God and the things of God. Think what would happen should you set aside ten minutes for spiritual realization! Only those who have been touched in some measure by the Spirit of God would have the capacity to sit for ten minutes in contemplative meditation. Think!

[6] Matthew 16:13, 15, 16.
[7] Matthew 23:9.
[8] John 10:30.
[9] Luke 15:31.

*"I and my Father are one." The Father has said to me, "Son, thou art ever with me, and all that I have is thine." Therefore, I have all that God has; all that God has is mine. "The earth is the Lord's, and the fulness thereof."*[10] *Of my own self I am nothing but, in this oneness with my Father, all that the Father hath is mine. "My peace I give unto you."*[11] *There is no limitation to the amount of peace that I have, because I have been given the Christ peace, the My peace. The Christ peace has been given unto me.*

Therefore, when the question is asked, "What have you in your house?" you can reply: "I have the full measure of Christ peace. I have all that the Father has, for the Father has given His allness unto me. God has even breathed into me His life, so I have in my consciousness life eternal. The Christ has come that I might have life, and that I might have it abundantly. Therefore, I have in my house—in my consciousness—abundant life, infinite life, eternal life, because this Christ has said, 'I am eternal life.' Therefore, I have eternal life in my consciousness as the gift of God. I have an infinity of supply because the Christ reveals: 'Your heavenly Father knoweth that ye have need of all these things,'[12] and 'it is your Father's good pleasure to give you the kindgom.'[13] Therefore, I have the kingdom of God within me, which is the kingdom of all that I shall ever need. I have in my consciousness eternal life, infinite supply, divine peace. The peace which passeth understanding I have.''

[10] Psalm 24:1.
[11] John 14:27.
[12] Matthew 6:32.
[13] Luke 12:32.

As you contemplate these principles for five or ten minutes each day, you carry into your world the awareness of the presence of all that God is and all that God has as a gift that has been bestowed upon you by the grace of God.

Your having contemplated these truths is the reason there is peace in our midst. You have brought "the peace of God, which passeth all understanding."[14] If there is love here with us, you have brought the love that is without limit. If there is supply, you have brought God's storehouse. All that the Father has is yours, and you have brought it here. Remember this: What you have brought here to make of this room a temple of God, you also bring to your business or to your home by your morning contemplation of this truth. You thereby make of your home a temple of God. You do not find love in your home: you bring love *to* your home, because love is found only where you express it. In other words, if your family is to find love, they will find it because you, who are attuned to God, bring it there. You who have been led to a spiritual teaching have been given the grace to know this truth, whereas members of your family and your business associates who are represented by "the natural man who receiveth not the things of God" cannot bring peace and harmony into their relationships.

Only those who have the Spirit of God indwelling are children of God. Only those who have the Spirit of God indwelling have been given the "peace which passeth understanding." Therefore, remember: What you discover here at this moment you have brought. Likewise, what you find in your home, in your business, in the world is what you bring to your home, to your business, or to the world.

[14] Philippians 4:7.

What have you in your consciousness? This is the password for meditation: "What have I in my consciousness?"

*Of myself I have nothing, but by the grace of God "all things that the Father hath are mine[15] . . . the earth is the Lord's, and the fulness thereof."[16] Therefore, I have been given My peace, the Christ peace. I have been given all these added things because my heavenly Father knoweth that I have need of them and it is His good pleasure to fulfill me. I am filled full of the grace of God and, by the grace of God, all that the Father hath is mine.*

*If you ask Me, I can give you bread; eating it, you will never hunger. I can give you living waters; drinking, you will never thirst.*

This is what you are saying in your household, in your business, in the world—only you are saying it silently and secretly. You never voice it openly because the command of the Master is that we do our praying in secret, where no man can hear us or see us. If your praying is done in the inner sanctuary of your consciousness, what the Father seeth or heareth in secret is shouted from the housetops. "Thy Father which seeth in secret himself shall reward thee openly."[17] Silently and sacredly ask yourself: "What have I in the house?"

*I have the grace of God. All that the Father hath is mine. I have been given quietness and confidence and stillness; I have been given My peace. The Father hath*

---

15 John 16:15.
16 Psalm 24:1.
17 Matthew 6:4.

*breathed His life into me, therefore I have God's life
which is eternal and immortal.*

   *I have that mind in me which was also in Christ
Jesus, and so I have no human desires and I seek nothing
of any man. "I and my Father are one," and I receive
all that I require because my Father knoweth my needs,
and it is His good pleasure to give me the kingdom.
Because I already have all, I pray only for the opportunity to share that which the Father hath given to me.*

Note what transpires in your home, in your business, and
in the world as you silently, sacredly, and secretly remind
yourself:

   *Thank God I ask nothing of any man except that we
love one another. I ask only the privilege of sharing
God's allness which is already mine. Why should I
look to "man, whose breath is in his nostrils,"*[18] *when
by right of divine sonship I am heir to all of the heavenly riches!*

Do you not see why there is an atmosphere of peace among
us? We came here for the purpose of abiding in the presence
of God and to tabernacle with the Spirit of God which is within
you and within me. We are gathered together to share the
spiritual grace of God, the spiritual presence of God and
the spiritual love of God. That is why there is peace with us;
there can be no such peace where people come to *get* something. When you sit down to meditate, turn quietly within
and realize:

[18] Isaiah 2:22.

*As the branch is one with the tree, as the wave is one with the ocean, so am I one with God. The allness of Infinity is pouring Itself forth into expression as my individual being, as my individual consciousness, as my individual life. Having received the allness of God, I want only to share it.*

As you resume your outer activity, you remember to have a ten-second meditation as often as possible, in which to remind yourself:

*The grace of God is upon me. I have spiritual meat and spiritual bread to share with all who are here, and those who accept it will never hunger. I can give to the world spiritual water, and those who accept this living water will never thirst. "I and my Father are one," and the Father is pouring Its allness through me, to you, and to this world.*

A contemplative meditation has in it something of a back-and-forth nature. You are virtually saying to the Father:

*Thank You, Father, that Your grace is upon me. Thank You, Father, that You have given me Your peace. If I have any hope, or faith, or confidence, You have given it to me. Of my own self I am nothing, so whatever measure of peace, hope, faith, and confidence I have is the gift of the Father within me. Thank You, Father, for Your grace, Your peace, Your abundance.*

You then pause, as if the still small voice were about to speak to you. It is an attitude of "Speak, Lord; for thy servant heareth."[19] If you persist in this way of life, eventually you

---

[19] 1 Samuel 3:9.

will discover that the Father *will* speak to you, and usually in this manner:

> *Son, I have been with you since before Abraham was. Know ye not that "I am with you alway, even unto the end of the world"?[20] Know ye not that "I will never leave thee, nor forsake thee"?[21] If you mount up to heaven, I will be there with you. Turn and recognize Me even in hell. If you walk through the valley of the shadow of death, I will not leave you.*
>
> *Turn within and seek Me. Acknowledge Me in the midst of you, and I will change death into life, age into youth, lack into abundance. Only abide in this Word and consciously let Me abide in you. Whither do you think you can flee from My Spirit?*

Open your consciousness and feel the peace which passes understanding where you are.

> *My peace give I unto you — My peace. My kingdom, the kingdom of Allness, is established within you. Abide in this truth and let this truth abide in you. Consciously remember that the son of God indwells you and that It is closer to you than breathing and nearer than hands and feet. "I can do all things through Christ which strengtheneth me.[22] . . . I live; yet not I, but Christ liveth in me."[23] Let Me, this indwelling son of God, abide in you.*

[20] Matthew 28:20.
[21] Hebrews 13:5.
[22] Philippians 4:13.
[23] Galatians 2:20.

If you have been led to a spiritual way of life, you will not have the capability to forget your ten-second meditations and your ten-minute contemplative meditations. If the Spirit of God dwells in you, you will be as unable to go through the hours of the day and night without the conscious remembrance of the presence of God as you would be unable to go without food. As food is necessary to the "natural man," so the conscious awareness of the presence of God is vital to the spiritual man. Spiritual food is essential to the son of God.

Silently and secretly make this acknowledgment to your family, to your business acquaintances, and to your neighbors: "I can give you living waters." Witness to what degree this changes the trend of your thought from being the "man of earth" who is always seeking to get something to being the spiritual son of God who is motivated by the desire to give and to share: "Ask of me, and I can give you the peace that passeth understanding. I can share with you the indwelling Christ peace which the Father hath given me."

Witness how this reverses the trend of your life. Whereas the natural man receiveth not the things of God because he is too busy seeking the baubles of "this world," the spiritual man is not only always receiving but he is sharing. He is able to discern that these spiritual treasures cannot be hoarded: they must always be expressed and allowed to flow from the within to the without. And so you secretly and sacredly carry them into your home and into your business, and then you take the next step and let them flow to your enemy.

> *"Father, forgive them; for they know not what they do."*[24] *If you ask Me, I will give you living waters, and you will never thirst again. I will give you meat,*

24 Luke 23:34.

*and you will never again hunger. I am come that you
might have life, and that you might have it more
abundantly.*

As you practice contemplative meditation, think what
is pouring through you to this world to help establish peace
on earth. There has not been peace on earth because so many
individuals have been seeking it, and few there are who have
sought to bring it, to express it, to share it. If there is to be
peace on earth, the Master clearly reveals that you and I must
bring it—and this *I* is the *I* of you, the divine Son of you. If
there is to be peace in the world, *you* must bring it—just as
you brought it here and as you are learning to carry it into your
home and into your business activity. Peace is not here until
you bring it. What have you in your consciousness?

*I have the peace that passeth understanding, and I
can carry it wherever I will, wherever I am, because in
God's presence there is fulfillment. The place whereon
I stand is holy ground because Christ dwelleth in me.
The indwelling Christ is the fulfillment, and where the
Christ is there is peace. Therefore I bring peace to my
body, I bring peace and quiet to my mind, and I bring
peace, quiet, love, and abundance to you, whoever the
"you" may be. I bring to you the grace of God. Go thou
and do likewise!*

# The Easter
## of Our Lives

IT IS THE DAY of the Crucifixion, and the Master is seated by himself somewhat apart from the people in the court-yard. Outside the gates the crowd has gathered. These are the multitudes whom Jesus fed when they were an-hungered; these are the people whom he healed of their diseases, of their sins, and of their infirmities. Some of them he even raised from the dead. Now they have gathered to make sure that he is cruci-fied. They have been lulled to forgetfulness of the good that they witnessed in his ministry, and evidently their ecclesias-tical authorities have convinced them that Jesus meant to destroy their temple, their religion, even their God. The fact that they saw the healings and experienced them is forgotten in the cry, "Crucify him! Crucify him!"

The Roman authorities are much concerned, because they have nothing against the man Jesus; they have nothing against his teaching; and they have no liking for the work of the day.

This the Master understands. He knows that on one side are the representatives of the Roman law, who have no desire to perform their unpleasant task, while on the other side are the ungrateful people whom he has blessed.

So he has a right to do a little thinking, and we have the right to look into his mind and to speculate as to what he is thinking. Could it be as he sits there waiting for the inevitable that he is saying to himself, "What a great spiritual victory has been given me! What a great revelation from on high, a revelation so great that I know that the words which I have spoken will never pass away. Some day men will remember them and repeat them, and these words will lift those who hear out of the grave of sin, disease, and death.

"What a wonderful light God has given me! What grace I have received from on high that I should know the meaning of all things, past, present, and future. With this great light I have brought healing, consolation, and comfort, not only to those of my present age, but even before Abraham was, those who existed will receive this light. Unto eternity will it brighten the lives of men. It will overcome the world: the world of war; the world of disease; the world of fear; and the world of sin. Yes, God has been very good to me; God has blessed me."

Alone in the courtyard, he remembers the love he has poured out on the world. In that remembrance, he must marvel at his own aloneness and ask, "With all my success, wherein has been my failure, if there is a failure? Wherein have I failed? Where are those I taught? Where are my disciples? Where are the apostles? Where are the twelve? Where are the seventy? Where are the two hundred? Where is my mother? Where are my brethren? Where are those who have been raised from the dead? Where are those who are to carry the message out into

the world? Have I so failed that God has given me this great
light and I have not been able to give it even to one of these?

"I placed my trust in Peter, in John, in Matthew, in Judas.
What has become of them? What has become of me that I
should not be able to inspire them with this great light which
I have received? Wherein is my failure? Where is the man
Lazarus? His sister Mary is here, outside the gate. She stands
by with love and adoration, as does the other Mary, she who
was taken in adultery. These two bear my burden with me.
But those others of whom I have the right to expect devotion
and sacrifice, those I have lost. They were my sheep, but I have
lost them. Even my mother doesn't seem to know me, to
recognize my work, or to understand my mission. My brothers,
little children with whom I grew up, with whom I played, and
who saw me when my eyes were first opened to the revelation
of God, even they seem not to know me.

"How is it that in all this wide world, none to whom I
have poured out myself, my message, my mission, compre-
hends it? Have I failed? The message hasn't failed; the mission
hasn't failed, because it came from on high. I am not deceived.
No one can tell me that this isn't the Christ-message, because
by its fruits I know it: the sick are healed; the dead are raised;
to the poor the gospel is preached. But why is it that I have
raised up no one to carry on, no one to understand it, not even
one to stand by and say, 'Well done, good and faithful servant.'
No, there is no one!"

So the Master ponders the lack of receptivity and respon-
siveness in the people whom he has blessed. The louder the
noise grows outside, the louder the clamor for his life, the
greater must be his astonishment that in this hour of inevitability, no human being stands beside him. Somewhere between
this moment of introspection and the moment when he is led

out to the Crucifixion, the light, which enabled him to endure the Crucifixion, to rise from the tomb, and to complete his mission in the ascension, dawns in his consciousness. This influx of light brings the realization that man whose breath is in his nostrils never has, cannot now, and never will comprehend the spiritual message, the mission of the Christ. Always those to whom we pour out ourselves and give of ourselves must be the very ones to turn and rend us. That must inevitably be, because there is that in the human mind which does not want to be extinguished. That is the secret. That is the mystery.

Watch this fact, that there is that in the human mind which does not wish to be extinguished. It is that something called "I," the human I, which boasts of its power, its wisdom, its understanding, and its goodness. This I is unwilling to be extinguished; it does not want to say, "Why callest thou me good? There is but one good, the Father in heaven." It does not want to admit, "I of mine own self can do nothing; the Father doeth the works." No! It likes to boast, "Just see how great is my understanding; see how great is my spirituality; see how great is my goodness." When a message teaches that human beings of themselves are not good, that they are not spiritual, that mortals are not the sons of God, but that they must die daily and be re-born of the Spirit—when a teaching such as that is presented to the world, it is then that antagonism is aroused; it is then that the fawning mob becomes belligerent, and that gratitude gives way to the cross, the nails, and the sword. Feed the multitudes, and they become the admiring throng; heal them, and they honor us by putting the robe and crown on us. But when they are told that they must deny themselves and recognize God as the reality of being, then there comes the experience of the crucifixion.

As the Master ponders this, there is again that repeated question, "Then have I failed? Did I fail?"; and from somewhere deep within his own being comes the answer, "You could not succeed and you could not fail, because this is not your work. This is *My* work, you are *My* instrument. Did you not tell the people that if you spoke of yourself you bore witness to a lie, that this message was not yours but His that sent you? Now remember that, at this moment. You cannot fail, because you never had a message, and you never had a mission. You are the instrument through which this word of truth is given to the world. Your part has been fulfilled. Now comes the greatest revelation that you have ever had, and it is this: all that appears as human experience is but an illusion. You are destined to prove the greatest revelation, that even death is an illusion. This is the highest revelation ever given to the world, the revelation that ultimately will be its salvation. Death in its most cruel form is an illusion. Out of this will come your resurrection and your ascension, and out of its accompanying disgrace will come the crowning glory of your divine sonship.

"How then can you fail, since in this victory you bear witness to the impotence of hate and jealousy, and to the great truth of the illusory nature of all evil? In one experience you annihilate the entire belief that the human mind, with its iniquity, its wickedness, its ingratitude, and forgetfulness, is a power. Regardless of their depth, you show the nothingness of ingratitude, jealousy, envy, and malice. You prove to the world of the sons of God that none of these things can ever destroy the life, harmony, wholeness, message, or mission of divinity."

This was the conversation and the debate which the Master had with himself. There was the question, "Why did these men forsake me? Why did they not receive my message?'' and there was the answer, the answer which came to Jesus during this debate with himself: "I have finished the work Thou hast given me to do. I have proved, once and for all time to come, that in the deepest degree—and there is no deeper degree of human iniquity than for a friend to betray his friend, for a student to betray his teacher, for the disciple to betray his master—I have proved in this experience that even that deepest degree of iniquity, even that, is not power."

The celebration of Easter is not to commemorate an event which took place two thousand years ago, but to reveal a principle; so that when we face a world filled with wickedness in high places, whether they be high spiritual places, high political places, or high commercial places, we can know the impotence of human scheming, human planning, human ambition, evil, degradation, and iniquity. We can stand fast in the faith that God, Itself, is our power, God, Itself, is our presence. It makes no difference what religious holidays we celebrate if we do not take from them the principle that they show forth. For us, the principle is all.

The Master never asked for recognition or for gratitude from the world for the work that he did, but there must have been a hope, an anticipation, that those who heard his message would stand firm in the faith and carry it forward. And from this experience of his, we can learn that God is the bearer of Its own message and needs no human agency. God needs no human Messiah. God needs no human disciples. Whether or not there is a spiritual teacher on the face of the earth, God will deliver to the consciousness of men the healing grace, the healing power. God, Itself, will speak the Word in the consciousness of men, and raise up seed, raise up the revelation and the understanding until the leaven works.

All of us have thought, at some time or other, that the carrying of the spiritual message was dependent upon a human avenue, and in that thought we have lost our healings, because we have accepted the belief that God must work through a person, thing, or thought. The Easter lesson is the high revelation that God works in us, and through us, without mediation. Never believe that without a book, a teaching, or right thinking, you can lose your demonstration; never believe that salvation is dependent on a man, on a thing, or on a thought. Watch the Master make the final demonstration after the loneliness of the Garden of Gethsemane, without the loyalty of disciples, without the benefit of human aid, even without the help of human thought. He stood alone in Christ, alone with God. There was not a single disciple to watch with him for one hour. Nevertheless, then as always, we see that with every human aid removed, "I and my Father are one." It is only in this realization of oneness, only in this realization of I-ness that the experience of resurrection and ascension can take place: " 'I and my Father are one.' I and the Father ascend and descend from the cross; I and the Father are buried in the tomb; I and the Father walk out of the tomb. Finally, I and the Father ascend above human sight in the realization of oneness, unity, completeness, perfection."

There will come a time in our own experience when we are in that courtyard, and when we know that before us lies inevitability in one form or another. Before us stands the desertion of everything and everyone upon whom we have placed reliance, and we find ourselves alone with God. It is in that aloneness with God that we find the spiritual reality of wholeness and completeness.

But this cannot be seen unless it can be seen, too, that the mission of the Master was not merely to multiply loaves and fishes, nor was it to transform physical bodies from sickness to health, nor to raise them from the dead. The mission of the Master was to take us into a new dimension of life in which we find spiritual reality. Bereft of temporal aids, of temporal good in any and every form, we find then and there the spiritual dimension, the spiritual reality of being—eternal, infinite, omnipresent—in which no true thing is ever lost. This is the highest phase of the Christ message and mission. Through it, we rise above human-ness, above human experience, above improving humanhood, into the revelation and realization of the kingdom of God. In the kingdom of God there is no loss, no lack, no limitation. In this kingdom within, the Master finds, not human beings to desert him, but angels to bear him up.

I bear witness to you that in proportion as our human dependencies depart from us, in proportion as we lose our faith in purely material means of help, their place is taken by angels, guardians from on high, from the infinite consciousness deep within—and we find a new world and a new life.

The only reason that we have the symbolic teaching of a Master deserted by his disciples is to show us that wherever our human trust has been, we must be prepared for that desertion; so that we can take the higher step of witnessing the spiritual aid, the spiritual wisdom, the spiritual angels, which are sent to us and which never leave us nor forsake us. Remember, "I will never leave you; I will never forsake you." This is not a man talking; this is an angel, a guardian angel, God's own witness within our consciousness, saying that if mother or father desert us, *It* will never leave us. We know through this symbolic lesson that there is That which did not desert the Master, and which enabled him to reveal to the world that the desertion of human help leads to that elevation of consciousness necessary to the realization of divine help.

It is not necessary that we be crucified; it is not necessary that our friends or relatives forsake us or that we be betrayed. That lesson was an extreme one to illustrate the fact that we must not place our faith in human avenues. If we do so, one of these days the medicines will not heal, the banks will not loan, and the friends will not stand by. But if through the Master's revelation we begin here and now to give up our dependency on disciples, on relatives, on friends, on capital, or on investments, then we shall find that we are picked up by angels, by spiritual power. Spiritual power! Do we really know, do we really believe that there is such a thing as spiritual power? Are we aware of the spiritual power which is called angels, guardians, or messengers from on high, which are no more or less than realizations of the divine Presence and Power within us? Do we know that this Power is more real than the disciples, the friends, and the relatives on the outer plane? The entire mission of the Master was to reveal that there are guardian angels—that around us are the everlasting arms. Are we willing to recognize that there is an unseen Presence and Power, upon which we can rely with greater faith than on anything in the visible?

What I want you to see from this Easter unfoldment is that this invisible Presence, Power, or Force is able to pick us up, but that It can do that only as we avail ourselves of It, as we release our hold on earthly powers. The Infinite Invisible does not reach us and does not take over while we are relying on that which is visible, finite, and temporal. Only as we release our mental hold on these, only as we give up our faith and trust in the visible, does this invisible Power take over and reveal to us the inner world of reality.

Remember, the Master said very clearly, "My kingdom is not of this world." In that statement, you have the Easter lesson: "My kingdom is not of this world. My disciples did

not come to my aid; the people I healed and fed did not stand
by or even testify for me. But watch and you will see the
invisible angels, the invisible Power, which will enable me
to walk out of the tomb and ascend above all mortal discord.
Human beings will betray; human power will fail; but I can
call on angels. Yes, I can call on angels. Watch these angels
pick me up. Watch them lift me from the cross and take me
from the tomb. That is the glory of the Father's message. That
is what the Father has been trying to say through me, and you
have not seen it. Have ye eyes and do not see? Have ye ears
and do not hear? I am bringing you a message, not of greater
good in this kingdom, but of a Power and of a Presence from
the invisible kingdom. My kingdom is not of this world. I
have overcome this world. Within me is this divine Presence,
this tremendous Force, and I tell you of it. My message is to
tell you that within you is the kingdom of God—not out there
in personal dependencies, not out there in faith upon crutches
that break, but within you. You have seen my disciples desert
me. You have seen those I healed and fed leave me alone.
Now I will show you the Invisible. Stand still and watch Its
power."

Remember that the emphasis of this message is on the
Infinite Invisible and on developing a consciousness of dependence on that which is not seen, on that which is not visible
out here. In my own experience I have witnessed that the inner
Light shines only in proportion to my withdrawal from the
outer world—not by my leaving the world, or its pleasures
and joys; but by my leaving my dependence upon it, by my
discarding my faith in person, place, or thing. We may think
this makes us stand alone. We may think that in his hour of
desertion and betrayal the Master stood alone. This is not true.
The Master never was betrayed and never was deserted, except

by the unreal personal sense. The Master was always in the company of the children of God, on earth and on the cross. At no time in his minstry did the Master walk alone. On the mountain top, although he appeared to be alone, in his realization of the unreal nature of the outer world, he communed with the children of God. He showed his disciples on the Mount of Transfiguration that the prophets were there with him; they were with him on the cross; they were with him in the tomb. When we seem most alone, we are most heavily engaged in divine company.

We can prove this for ourselves. Let us say that you have gone home, and have slept for two or three or four hours, and then have awakened. You get out of bed and stay awake by yourself for a while. Watch how you find yourself in divine company, how you lose all sense of friendlessness, of lack and limitation. The weariness of the world is gone. In the stillness of the night, we find ourselves alone, as was the Master in the garden. And so, as we commune with our own inner being, very soon we will find out why the Master could find the great Hebrew masters keeping company with him, and why he could stay forty days or forty nights alone. He was not alone. He was in divine companionship.

And then when you return to the world, and walk the streets, and take care of your business, you will begin to learn the meaning of a Presence which walks with you, a Presence which walks beside you, a Presence which walks behind you. This Presence will be a joy to you, as It has been to me; It will even say: "Up to now I have walked behind or beside you. Now I am *in* you"; and then you will know that there is no such thing as betrayal and desertion. There is only the unreal picture of an illusory world to fool you and tempt you to believe in the reality of evil power. The one reality is God, expressing Itself in individual life as divine companionship, divine protection, divine supply—all emanations from the Infinite Invisible. It is this Infinite Invisible which never leaves us nor forsakes us; It has been with us since before Abraham was, and It will be with us until the end of the world.

As our attention and thought are drawn away from those we think we have humanly helped, or from those who humanly owe us an obligation, we find ourselves saying: "Whatever good I can be to you, let me be; but you owe me nothing for it." Then and only then do we realize that divine compensation, recognition, and reward are within. The guardian angel is always with us when we have withdrawn our gaze from without us.

Remember the Easter lesson: "My kingdom is not of this world." Remember that the greatest blessing that has come to the human world has been the denial of the Master by those he fed and healed, and by his very own disciples. The great lesson we must learn from the experience of Jesus is not to trust man whose breath is in his nostrils, not to place our faith in the outer world, but always to turn within and to become acquainted with our guardian angel, with the angel of the Lord, with our divine protector, with the very Christ of God, which has been planted in the midst of us since the beginning of all time.

Men have fashioned their human, temporal kingdoms out of gold, silver, brass, and clay. In the seventh chapter of Daniel we learn of the finite, temporary nature of these worldly kingdoms. Daniel tells us that a new kingdom will be set up which will never be destroyed. This kingdom is carved out of a stone, cut out of a mountain without hands! This stone destroys all temporal kingdoms, and the work of men. Think of this: a stone carved out of a mountain without hands! Is not this the work of God? And the kingdom that shall stand forever, is not that the reign and realm of the Christ, the Power that rules "not by might nor by power but by my spirit"? Human life, built upon gold, silver, brass, and iron mixed with clay, is a kingdom divided against itself. Spiritual wisdom alone, the still small voice, can destroy it and reveal the kingdom of immortality under the government of Love.

As faith and confidence in men, in metals, and in materials is displaced by the understanding of God as substance, the power and glory of the new consciousness appears. "My kingdom is not of this world." The ministering angels within our own consciousness, the impartations of the spiritual Word within by the voice of the Lord, make for the safety, security, harmony, joy, and peace of our world. The still small voice, which is the power of God, the only Power, thunders in the silence:

> Give unto the Lord, O ye mighty, give unto the Lord glory and strength.
> Give unto the Lord the glory due unto his name; worship the Lord in the beauty of holiness.
> The voice of the Lord is upon the waters: the God of glory thundereth: the Lord is upon many waters.
> The voice of the Lord is powerful; the voice of the Lord is full of majesty.
> The voice of the Lord breaketh the cedars; yea the Lord breaketh the cedars of Lebanon.
> He maketh them also to skip like a calf; . . . .
> The voice of the Lord divideth the flames of fire.
> The voice of the Lord shaketh the wilderness; . . . .
> The voice of the Lord maketh the hinds to calve, discovereth the forests; and in his temple doth every one speak of his glory.

*The Lord sitteth upon the flood; yea, the Lord sitteth King forever.*

*The Lord will give strength unto his people; the Lord will bless his people with peace.*

Now is come salvation, and strength, and the kingdom of our God, and the power of his Christ.

# A Lesson to Sam

Now, SAM, THIS LESSON is important because it is
not just a lesson for one day. If you are faithful in putting this
into practice, it will be sufficient for the rest of your life, even
if you never receive another lesson from me.

I have been thinking about your going away to school and
of how you will be able to live The Infinite Way when you are
away from our personal influence, your mother's and mine,
and when you may not do too much reading in my books.
While I hope that you will do some reading each day, if only
a page in one of my writings, even more would I like to have
you learn this lesson, which I am about to give you, so well
that, if you were alone on a desert island or out in a rubber
boat in the middle of the ocean and had no person around you
and no books with you, you could still survive and demonstrate your safety, your security, peace, food, clothing, hous-
ing, and everything necessary for your unfoldment.

I want to tell you the secret that has brought me happiness,
joy, success, prosperity, and the ability to be of help to my

fellow-man and to children throughout this world. I want you
to know that secret so that you can go and do likewise.

First of all, whenever you are faced with any problem,
whether it is one of health or one concerning your lessons at
school, or let us say one that concerns your relationship with
other boys in school or with your teachers, here is your first
step: Get comfortable; close your eyes; put your feet on the
floor; and now remember that God is closer to you than
breathing, nearer than hands and feet. Right there, where you
are standing or sitting or playing, God is. You have only to
close your eyes, get quiet for a moment, and God will solve
your problem.

It may sound strange to you that you don't have to tell
God what your problem is or that you don't have to ask God
for any favors, and that you don't even have to make any
statements or affirmations. All you have to do is to close your
eyes, get still for a moment, and realize that God is as close
to you as inside your own chest. Then be patient for a few
minutes, and the Spirit, Itself, will take over. If you need help
with your lessons, that instruction will come forth very quickly, just as you have seen here in our work together that, when
you have been stuck with a mathematical problem, instead of
my working it out for you, we meditated. And then when you
went back to your book, you found the answer as plainly stated
there as if it had been written out especially for you.

So it is, if you have a problem in your studies or if there
is some subject that you are not properly grasping, stop what
you are doing for a moment, close your eyes, and realize God
right here, closer to you than breathing. Wait for just a minute
or two, and you will find that God, who is the divine Intelligence of your being, knows that you are coming to Him and
what you are coming to Him for. Always remember that it is

God's good pleasure to give you the answer. In fact, it is very much like a radio station: God is always talking to you; God is always revealing the answer to every problem, whether it concerns your lessons, your health, or your human relationships; but you cannot receive God's guidance, direction, protection, or support unless you are tuned in to accept it.

It is like your sitting here in this room and receiving instruction in spiritual wisdom from me. But suppose that you had your ears closed and weren't listening, or suppose you were outside playing, or suppose you were downtown at the movies, how then could you receive that which I so willingly offer you? The answer is: You couldn't.

Now, as a human father, I would gladly give you every spiritual secret I have, just as readily as I would give you every dollar I have, if these would prove a blessing to you. But do you not see that I cannot give you any of these things unless you are receptive to them, unless you are giving back in return your attention, your gratitude, your love, and your obedience?

Just so it is with God. You must give God obedience, attention, lovingness—not by loving a God whom you cannot see, but by loving the boys and girls with whom you come in contact, and your teachers. Always remember, as you leave this home, that you are to express the same respect toward the boys and girls whom you meet as the mutual respect that you have witnessed taking place in this home. You know the love and respect there is between your mother and me and between you and me; and you know that, when your mother and I go out into the world, we give this same love and this same respect to everyone we meet. That is the example you must follow and carry out into practice. And why? In order that you may receive God's grace because, even though God is present with you, you cannot receive God's grace unless love, joy, and respect fill your mind and your Soul.

Each one of us is responsible for himself. There is no God sitting up in a sky, looking down upon you and judging your actions; but there is a God-center within you that knows everything you do and which brings back to you that which you send out. Therefore, the love and the respect that you send out are the love and respect that you get back, and not only that, but they are pressed down and running over.

Now even though you went out into the world and loved your neighbor as yourself and were humanly good in every way, this would not be enough, for that is only fulfilling the Ten Commandments, and what you are now being taught is how to fulfill the Sermon on the Mount.

The Infinite Way is really a revelation which says that you do not have to speak to God, but that you must have periods of the day or the night when you listen to God; and even though you may not hear a voice, remember that just by opening your ear to God and being silent for a minute or two you have permitted God to rush into that vacuum which you have created.

It operates like this: Close your eyes; put your feet on the floor; listen way down inside of yourself; and then remember that this day which lies ahead of you is now God-governed, God-protected, God-maintained, and God-sustained because you have consciously opened your consciousness to the presence and the government of God. Remember that, if you do not do this every morning, you go out into the world just as a human being, subject to all the trials and tribulations of the human world, and without divine guidance.

Actually at your age and with the teaching that you have

had here in your home, you should be ready to have four periods a day—early in the morning, at noon, about dinner time, and before retiring—in which to take two minutes each time just to sit down and turn within and say, "Here I am, Father; speak Lord, Thy servant heareth. I am obedient to Thy will." And then just be still for one minute. I can promise you that if you do that, your life in school will be a success, and even more than that, you will be laying the foundation for a completely God-governed life.

What the world does not always understand is that it is not too important whether or not you go through church rituals or church forms or ceremonies. A church can be helpful if you go to it with your mind open: It can be an opportunity for you to be quiet and hear the still small voice. Therefore, I say to you that if the boys in your school go to a church service, I would certainly suggest that you also go to the service—and remember, this is only a suggestion, for your life is free for you to make or to break—and if they go through a ritual, you go through it; if they go through forms of worship, you go through them. Because you are all united in that service in the name of God, it can do you a great deal of good; but the real good comes because you are there to acknowledge God's grace and God's glory.

The important thing that I want you to see, Sam, is that, in any instance and in every instance, at any moment of the day or night, God is instantly available to you merely by closing your eyes and inwardly listening. I'm trying to emphasize that it isn't the statements you make, it isn't talking to God, it isn't asking God. None of that is necessary because the secret that I have learned is that God is infinite intelligence and He already knows our needs, even before we do. The way God fulfills our needs is through our inner listening—

not through our talking, not through our saying words or thinking thoughts, because the Master said, "Take no thought for your life, what ye shall eat; neither for the body, what ye shall put on . . . Your Father knoweth that ye have need of these things . . . for it is your Father's good pleasure to give you the kingdom." Do you see that?

It is His good pleasure to give you the kingdom, and God does not even hold you in punishment for your sins. Even though you make a mistake, even though you commit a sin, if you are truly repentant in the sense that you realize that you have sinned and that it wasn't right, in that instant you are forgiven. You do not carry around the penalty any longer than you carry around the obstinacy of believing you are right when you know in your heart and Soul you are wrong. Do you understand that? You cannot go around and do wrong and not acknowledge it to yourself and expect that you can receive God's grace.

You receive God's grace every time you acknowledge within yourself, "I know I've done wrong," or perhaps, "I don't know that I've done wrong, but if I have, wipe it out, because it wasn't intentional. I never mean to do wrong, but always want to do unto others as I would have others do unto me." In that way, you purify yourself. I have been healed of illnesses merely by asking God's forgiveness for my sins; and of course, my sins are not major ones because you know that is not our mode of living. But whatever it is—when we are guilty of holding people in criticism or condemnation, or when we are not loving enough or forgiving enough—we are sinning against the Holy Spirit. So it is a wholesome thing once in a while to go to God and say, "I realize that humanly I haven't been perfect; therefore, forgive my sins, forgive my trespasses, and let's start all over again."

In this way, Sam, you will learn the greatest lesson that I have ever learned, and that is that the place whereon I stand is holy ground. God is right here where I am, and God is available the very minute that I stop talking and stop thinking and turn within in humility, acknowledging God's grace, God's power, God's Spirit within me, and then relax for just a minute or two and let that Spirit take over. That really is all there is to the whole Infinite Way.

All the writings of The Infinite Way are only for the purpose of leading people to this revelation of God's omnipresence and ever availability, without taking thought, without words, without anything except the humility to sit or stand or lie down, close the eyes, and acknowledge, "I, of my own self, can do nothing. The Father within me doeth the works . . . Speak, Lord; for Thy servant heareth." Then wait just one minute or two minutes before you get up and go about your task. If you learn to practice this four times a day as I suggest, it will not be long before you realize that you are doing it many more than four times a day.

And now, just one thing more. Never forget that one of the greatest statements in the Bible is, "In all thy ways acknowledge him, and he shall direct thy paths." This means that, when you awaken in the morning, your first thought has to be, "Thank you, Father, for this glorious day that is before me." When you eat, you stop for that blink of the eyes, as you know we do here in the home, and even if all you say to yourself is, "Happy days," "Good appetite," or whatever it is that you want to say with your lips, you mean with your Soul, "Thank you, God, for setting this table." Right?

So it is, that when you go out to play, blink your eyes and realize, "Thank you, Father, for Thy presence." When you go swimming, when you participate in sports, when you do your homework, acknowledge God's presence there, and then you won't have to rely on your own ability because, if you do, I can tell you in advance that you will not be equal to it. I know because, alone, I am not equal to my job. If it were not for God's grace at every step that I take, this work that you witness here could not be done.

Well, Sam, I don't know that anyone could add anything to this, but if so, I'm sure that it will be done some day. I am going to have this typed for you so that you can read it over once in a while as a reminder. This is the secret of life and, with this that I am giving you now, you can carve out for yourself a grand life of service to others, a blessing to yourself, and a joy to your parents, and the whole thing for the glory of God.

Always remember, God made you, and therefore any good thing you do is to the glory of God. Your parents brought you into this expression and are your human guardians, supporting, supplying and protecting you, and on the human plane, every good thing you do becomes a glory to your parents, something in which they can take pride. And so, you have your spiritual Father, in whom you should glory and to whom you should give glory, and you have your human parents, to whom you should give the opportunity to glory in your accomplishments.